Praise for
Allie's Bayou Rescue,
Book One in the Princess in Camo Series

"*Allie's Bayou Rescue* is an awesome book to read together as mom and daughter! We love how real it was about the obstacles we face as girls—but not without a God who cares for us in our struggles, pursues us, and knows EXACTLY where we are going, AND HAS IT all under control—especially when we don't."

Elisabeth and Grace Hasselbeck, TV personality and
daughter … and Daughters of the One True King!!

D1166448

Dog Show Disaster

Other Books in the Princess in Camo Series

faithgirlz™

PRINCESS IN CAMO
Dog Show Disaster

By Missy and Mia Robertson

With Jill Osborne

ZONDER**kidz**

ZONDERKIDZ

Dog Show Disaster
Copyright © 2018 by Missy Robertson and Mia Robertson
Illustrations © 2018 by Mina Price

This title is also available as a Zondervan ebook.

Requests for information should be addressed to:
Zonderkidz, 3900 *Sparks Dr.* SE, *Grand Rapids, Michigan* 49546

Library of Congress Cataloging-in-Publication Data
ISBN 978-0-310762522

Art direction: Cindy Davis
Interior design: Denise Froehlich

Printed in the United States of America

18 19 20 21 22 /LSC/ 10 9 8 7 6 5 4 3 2 1

"Get rid of all bitterness, rage, anger, harsh words, and slander, as well as all types of evil behavior. Instead, be kind to each other, forgiving one another, just as God through Christ has forgiven you."

EPHESIANS 4:31 (NLT)

To my amazing husband who can't take a nap without a lapdog and a blanket and who doesn't let that effect his masculinity. You're the man, Babe!
—Missy

To Mamaw Kay for always teaching me that dogs are much more than just pets—they're lifelong companions.
—Mia

CHAPTER 1

Caught in the Act

H azel Mae!"
I sprinted down the dirt path in our neighborhood, that leads to the creek running behind my old house. That's exactly where I knew my silly, white poof-ball dog would be. Using her old backyard as a bathroom.

Lord, it's a beautiful Saturday morning. Please don't let Mad-girl be home and ruin it.

"Mad-girl," is none other than Madison Doonsberry, twelve-year-old daughter of Andrew Doonsberry, who happens to be the new owner of my old house.

Hazel Mae, being a dog, couldn't seem to understand that the house wasn't hers anymore, so she kept escaping from my cousin Kendall's house—my current residence—to, well . . . deposit nasty things on the Doonsberry's lawn.

Like I needed any more help getting Madison to hate me.

"Hazel Mae—don't you even *think* about it!" I spied her up in the distance, circling around her favorite grass patch. I pulled a plastic bag out of my sweatshirt pocket, and hurdled over the hedge so I could snatch her up before . . .

"Are you trespassing *again*, Allie Carroway?"

Mad-girl.

She crossed her arms, glared at me, and stuck her right hip out to the side.

"Am I going to have to call the homeowner's association this time and file a complaint? Or perhaps I should call my dad's film crew to come over. This would make a great episode for *Lunker Law*. Doonsberrys vs. Carroways. I bet ratings would skyrocket."

Madison's dad once lived in this part of the Louisiana bayou, but moved away thirty years ago. During that time, he became a high-powered lawyer in Florida, got married, and had two kids—twins Parker and Madison. Four months ago, he and his wife divorced, and he returned to Louisiana to star in a reality TV fishing show called *Lunker Law*. It's a great show. Informative, funny, and I would love it a *whole lot* more if it didn't air on another network at the same time as my family's show *Carried Away with the Carroways*.

Madison flipped her long, strawberry blonde hair behind both shoulders and smirked.

"It's okay, Hazel Mae. I don't blame you. These things are always the fault of negligent pet owners."

Hazel Mae—oblivious to my pain—finished up her business and ran around the lawn, wagging her tail, and chasing after a butterfly.

How can you be so happy in enemy territory?

"I'm really sorry, Madison. It won't happen again."

"Well, I seriously *doubt* that. I've seen your show. You bayou people have no discipline."

"*Bayou* people?"

I reached down with the plastic bag to pick up Hazel Mae's mess. When I stood back up, my head started pounding.

Gee, I wonder if I have the discipline to hold on to this bag? It feels like it wants to fling itself toward Mad-girl.

It took all my *bayou* self-control to put the bag down on the grass instead.

"Yes, bayou people! Everyone knows about your disasters." Madison opened her hand and began to count "disasters" off

on her fingers. "Let's see, you had a goat loose in the house, frogs jumping around in the laundry room, your brother practically blew the place up on the Fourth of July, and didn't your dad bring a beaver in one time? Seriously, Allie, I don't even like to think of all the horrible messes you've made in my house."

"It was *my* house for twelve years," I said.

"And it's a wonder it's still standing."

I took a deep breath, and blew it out.

Count to ten, Allie. One . . . two . . . ten. Okay.

I forced a grin.

"It's a nice house, Madison. If it weren't for my allergies, we'd still be in it."

Gah. Why did I have to say *that*? No need to give her any more ammunition.

"Well, Allie-Allergy, you'll be happy to know that we enlarged your teeny-tiny room. I honestly don't know how you managed to breathe in that little space. And, I half-expected to find dead rats in the wall when we tore it down."

Hazel Mae finally chased the butterfly in my direction, so I scooped her up.

"Gotcha, you little fur ball." I turned back toward Madison. "You tore a wall down?"

She smiled and flipped her hair some more.

"Made two rooms into one. Added new carpet, crown molding, and even put in a bay window. The place just needed someone with class to make improvements."

"*Class*?" Now my blood was boiling.

Lord, help me not to say something I'm going to regret.

I opened my mouth, and began to say something I would regret. "Listen, if you think . . ."

Thankfully, Madison interrupted. "Speaking of class, you go to Ouachita Middle School, right?"

Madison came over and started petting Hazel Mae.

"Be careful. She's a *bayou* dog. She could have fleas or ticks, and she's known to have really bad breath."

Madison didn't respond to that. She looked at me with her cloudy green eyes.

"Well, do you? Go to OMS?"

I shrugged. "Yeah, I go there."

"Then we might be in the same class starting Monday."

"But I thought you went to that private school."

Madison looked away, but kept petting Hazel Mae.

"Yeah, well that didn't work out. Parker and I are transferring."

Great. My enemy not only lives in my old house, but now she's going to my school.

I gulped. "Do you know what teacher you have for homeroom?"

Please, don't say Mrs. Mellon.

"It's Miss Lewis, I believe," Madison said. "Parker has a Mrs. Mellon. It's the first time we've ever been in different classes."

Good news for me, and bad news for you, Mad-girl.

"Is Miss Lewis nice?" Madison pulled her hand away from Hazel Mae and bit her lip.

I stepped back and focused my gaze on Mad-girl's furrowed brow. "Well, everyone has their own opinion of Miss Lewis. I think I'll just let you make up your own mind." I grinned, and held up a hand to wave goodbye, and good-riddance. "See you on Monday!"

CHAPTER 2

Donuts and Dilemmas

Hazel Mae, did you hear that? Mad-girl is coming to my school! How am I supposed to survive that? There should be a law that designates Doomsberry-free zones."

"Doomsberry" is the nickname that my Mamaw Kat gave to Madison's dad when he was a kid. I guess he was a rascal, always hanging around her house causing trouble—including stealing some valuable heirloom tablecloths out of the storage shed and making tents out of them.

I gave Madison the nickname Mad-girl. I've never called her that to her face, it's just my little private joke—because she *always* seems to be mad.

At least she is at me. And, besides losing track of Hazel Mae a few times which resulted in a mess on the Doonesberry lawn, I've never done anything to deserve her anger. If anything, I should be mad at *her* for always referring to me as "bayou people" (like it's a bad thing), for making fun of the house I love, and for always rubbing it in that her dad's show ratings are higher than my family's show ratings. For now.

I huffed and puffed my way through the neighborhood—which is made up of houses that mostly belong to my family members. It had always been so peaceful here—until Madison Doonsberry moved in.

I looked down at Hazel Mae, who had her tongue hanging out, panting.

"I guess you're not going to give me any advice, are you? Must be nice to be a dog sometimes."

I jogged up and over the small hill in the middle of our park-like neighborhood and ran down the trail to our brand-new Carroway cousin clubhouse—The Lickety Split. I stopped and stared at the newly-stained wood building, situated way up in a tree, with a roomy balcony and a twisted branch railing. If this were a movie, there would have been angels singing in the background of this scene.

It was a beautiful sight.

And—it's a Doomsberry-free zone!

The Lickety Split took the place of our old clubhouse—the Diva Duck Blind. The Diva had been painted pink and purple—a real girl hangout. But everything changed a few months ago when Kendall's family adopted twelve-year-old Hunter. We did what any group of loving cousins would do—we changed the clubhouse to be more boy-friendly—but not until we had a little "initiation fun" with Hunter. Well, we *thought* it would be fun, but then there was a storm, and the lights went out, the river flooded, we lost Hunter, and a gator tried to eat my cousin Ruby. That's all. Initiations in the bayou can be intense. But, since we're "bayou people," we survived, and then we tore down the Diva—which we found out was full of mold—and constructed The Lickety Split.

I had taken three steps up the spiral staircase when a brunette head with a pink streak popped over the balcony railing and yelled down.

"Oh, good, you're here early. I have something to show you."

It was my cousin, Lola.

"Early?"

And then I remembered. It was almost time for our weekly "Donuts-in-the-Split" cousin meeting.

Hazel Mae ran up the stairs in front of me while I checked my phone. Nine-thirty. Why was Lola here so early?

I continued up the steps.

"Hazel Mae escaped and I had to catch her before she went on the Doonsberry's lawn again."

"Uh-oh." Lola put her hand to her mouth.

I nodded. "Yeah, I didn't get there in time either. And now I'm on Madison's list."

Lola waved me over to the wooden writing desk with the log legs that Hunter had built for the Split.

"Speaking of Madison, I need to ask you what I'm supposed to do about *this*."

She pointed to a turquoise envelope, covered in yellow daisies. Lola's name was written on the front.

Lola picked it up, opened it, and pulled out a stiff piece of cardstock that had those yellow daisies bordering words written in calligraphy:

YOU'RE INVITED

Madison Doonsberry's 13th Birthday Party

Saturday, April 1st, 4:00 pm

Swimming, Food, Games, and Sleepover

Hope you can come!

I read the whole invitation over and over. It was annoying seeing my old address on an invitation to someone else's party.

I looked up at Lola.

"Well, I can see why she likes you, since you're the fashionable one."

Lola scrunched her eyebrows together. "I don't know what to do. I'm the only one of us who got an invitation. Don't you think that's weird?"

"Ruby didn't even get one?"

"No. And she was standing right next to me when Madison handed me mine, so it's not like Madison forgot or anything."

Ruby is Lola's younger sister, but she looks like she could be related to Madison, with that red hair of hers. She just turned eleven, only a year younger than Lola, but she's sweet as pie, and everyone loves her. If anyone would get a birthday invitation, it would be Ruby.

"What did Madison say when she gave it to you? Did she mention *me* at all?"

Lola shook her head. "All she said was that she thought all her friends at private school would like me, and that she hoped I could come."

A voice called from below.

"I have fresh donuts!"

Ruby. This is another reason everyone loves her.

Lola walked out to the balcony, and I followed. "Ooh, Sis! I'm glad you're early!" Then Lola turned to me. "Ruby made the donuts from scratch this week! She was frying them up just a little while ago."

Every Saturday since we opened the Lickety Split, we've scheduled a ten o'clock, Donuts-in-the-Split meeting. We take turns bringing the donuts. Mine are always day-old, because I have Mom drive me by the donut shop on Friday after school. Ruby's weeks are the best.

"Why did you leave so fast?" Ruby, huffing and puffing from climbing the steps, handed the basket of donuts to Lola, who uncovered them and sniffed. "I wanted you to help me decorate them."

"I'm sorry, I had some things on my mind, so I wandered over." Lola pulled out a fresh donut that had light pink frosting and dark pink sprinkles. "Looks like this one's for me." She started to take a bite, but Ruby put her hand up to stop her. "Don't you think we should wait for everyone else?"

Lola stopped mid-bite and sighed. "You're right. But I hope they hurry."

"Everyone else" is my thirteen-year-old cousin Kendall—who I currently share a room with while waiting for my new "allergen-free" house to be built—and Hunter, the boy who always wears basketball shorts.

"Hey!" An out-of-breath voice sounded from the ground. Hunter. I looked over the railing at the top of his wavy, blonde head. He must have run the whole way. A sweat drip creeped down the side of his cheek, and his black, rectangular-framed glasses sat halfway down on his nose.

"I really wish we would reinstate passwords," Hunter said. "I loved mine."

"Gator Buster," was Hunter's password. We gave it to him temporarily, when we had the old Diva, since his middle name *is* Buster, and because part of his initiation was to prove that an old family story about a boy-eating gator living in Mamaw and Papaw's shed was false. Hunter proved it by sitting in that shed for an hour and not getting eaten, but then later—in the swamp—he ended up wrestling and then wrapping a gator's mouth closed with duct tape.

"Passwords are too exclusive," I said. "So we're not doing that anymore, remember? Re-read the proclamation we all signed on your way in."

"Okay! I love the agreement!"

I shook my head. You can't stop Hunter's enthusiasm.

As Hunter took a minute to read the framed proclamation

that hung on the wall next to the door, I watched my cousin-and-now-roomie, Kendall, stroll up the small hill toward the Lickety Split. It was funny to watch her change the angle of her head to point toward the breeze so that her straight brown hair could flow evenly back behind her shoulders.

She held Eleanor Rigby—her black miniature poodle that she rescued from the animal shelter. She took the name from a Beetle's song that talks about lonely people. One day last month, our Jr. high group from church went to help pull some weeds at the shelter, and then we all ventured in to see the pups. Ellie and Kendall hit it off immediately—and now Eleanor Rigby isn't lonely anymore.

Hazel Mae ran down the stairs when she spotted Ellie.

"Hey, you could have played with her at the house earlier, instead of escaping to Madison's house to get me in trouble," I said, chuckling a little.

"Kendall's here," I said. "We can start the meeting." I smiled and turned to enter the Lickety Split. We had a lot to talk about.

CHAPTER 3

Canine Carnival

"So, Allie . . ." Lola grabbed a donut hole from Ruby's basket, chomped a bite, and swallowed. "We all know you're going to be voted Student Project Manager for the carnival this year. What's the theme going to be?"

"It's not a done deal yet," I said. "I still have to give the speech on Monday. I may chicken out."

"Yeah, and the boys might not vote for her," Hunter said.

An orange "throw" pillow shot from Kendall's hand across the room to where Hunter sat on an orange Adirondack chair.

"Hey, I didn't say I wouldn't vote for her! We have a lot of boys at the school, that's all. You need to present a theme that they'll like too. So don't pick princesses or glitter ducks . . ."

I put my hand out. "How about dogs?"

Hunter's face lit up. "Dogs? That'll work. I love dogs. Most guys love dogs too!" Hunter's dog, a brown-and-white corgi named T-Rex, was adopted from the shelter just a few days after Kendall got Ellie.

Ruby smiled. "What *about* dogs?"

I petted Hazel Mae, who seemed to like the idea too. "Well, how about having a Canine Carnival and Dog Show, with all the proceeds going to the animal shelter? That place needs some upgrading."

Lola put both hands over her heart. "Oh, Allie, that's a beautiful idea. You'll be voted the Student Project Manager for sure with that one."

Every year, Ouachita Middle School holds an end-of-the-year carnival that benefits an organization in town. The faculty advisor for the project, Mrs. Mellon, who is the nicest, most caring teacher anyone has ever met, started the tradition ten years ago, during her very first year of teaching. The student body always elects an eighth-grader as the Student Project Manager for the event, and that student, who I hoped would be me, works with Mrs. Mellon, an appointed committee of students, and the rest of the kids at the school to pull off something spectacular.

But first I needed to give an outstanding speech, one that would get the students excited about my idea, and as I looked out at my amazing cousins, I decided they would have to be involved.

"So, I'm thinking that I need you all to help me with the speech."

Kendall put Ellie down and she looked at me through narrowed eyes. "I'm only really good at writin' songs . . ."

"I don't need you all to *write* it. I need you to be *in* it. With your dogs."

Hunter jumped up and pumped a fist in the air. "Oh, yeah! T-Rex will win the election for you."

All our dogs had come from the animal shelter. Ellie and T-Rex were the newest additions. Hazel Mae had been around for a few years, and Lola and Ruby had adopted twin chocolate labs, Max and Monet, from the shelter when they were puppies.

"Has T-Rex learned the Catapult yet?" I asked.

All Carroway dogs love jumping on the huge trampoline in Ruby and Lola's front yard. So, one day, we taught them all how to jump off a mini-trampoline through a hula hoop. Hazel Mae can do a roll and land on her feet. We call it the "Carroway Catapult."

Hunter scrunched up his face. "Not yet."

"Hmm." I crossed my arms, tapped my foot, and thought a minute. "Maybe T-Rex can add some comedy to the routine. I was thinking of having our dogs do the Carroway Catapult during my speech, and then I'll tell everyone that we're having a "Spectacular Dog Trick Competition" at the carnival. Anyone can enter, and we can offer to bring in a dog-training expert a few weeks earlier to show the kids some tricks they can teach their dogs. What do you think?"

"I love the idea!" Ruby said. "Max has been getting lazy. He needs to learn some new tricks."

"Would you like me to sew some pink bows for the dogs to wear for the big speech?" Lola asked. "Well, except for T-Rex and Max."

"How about some pink and green camo bandannas instead," I said. "And we'll meet later at your house to practice the Catapult to make sure they can all still do it."

"Sounds like a plan," Hunter said. Then he got up and walked over to the basket of donuts that Ruby had set on the writing desk.

"Hey, what's this?" Hunter held up Madison's birthday invite.

"Madison invited me to her birthday party," Lola said. "And I'm not sure what to do, since I'm the only Carroway she invited."

Hunter shrugged. "Why not go? I mean, she's new to the neighborhood, and she needs friends, right? Maybe she'll decide to like all of us if you're nice to her."

"I'm pretty sure she'll never like me," I said.

Hunter waved a finger in the air. "Never say never. She could end up being your best friend someday, Allie."

We were all quiet for a minute. Hunter's approach was

kind and sensible. But we *were* talking about Madison Doonsberry here!

Plus, can an enemy *ever* end up being your best friend?

I shook my head. "I don't know. Something smells fishy to me."

Hunter laughed. "Maybe it's because her dad stars in a fishing show!"

Hunter looked around at us like we were all crazy. "Oh, come on! Have you seen *Lunker Law*? It's hilarious! Last night, Mr. Doonsberry was talking about some unusual laws in Louisiana, like you can't have a fake wrestling match! So, he catches this huge catfish, right? And he flops around with it in the boat, and he keeps popping his head up and yelling, 'This is not fake! I'm really wrestlin' this fella!' I was dying laughing!"

Kendall shook her head. "Hunter, we were all downstairs watchin' *Carried Away with the Carroways* last night."

"Yeah," Lola said. "We thought you were up in your room doing homework."

"Oh. Well, it *was* Friday night, so I took a little break and turned my TV on."

"You should have come down with us," I said.

"But I already know what's on *our* show. I'm in it! Hey, speaking of that—aren't we supposed to film today?"

"What? We're filmin' on a Saturday?" Kendall popped up.

I pulled my phone from my back pocket and checked the call sheet.

"Picnic lunch. Mamaw and Papaw's house. Let's go!"

CHAPTER 4

Picnic Pests

Some people think that if you're in a reality TV show, cameras follow you around 24/7. But, *nobody* wants to experience *that* much of the Carroways.

So, instead, we have the cameras around more like 8/5. Eight hours a day, five days a week. Since the kids aren't in every scene, and we have to go to school, for us it's more like 4/3. And if something ridiculous happens when the cameras aren't rolling, we reenact it for the cameras later. So you don't miss the good stuff.

But on this particular Saturday, the cameras *were* rolling when the ridiculous happened.

Things were going smoothly. The scenes of us all debating about the best picnic lunch foods were hilarious. And the "super-long hike" we all took down to the river's edge near Mamaw and Papaw's was made not-so-boring by Hunter, who kept forgetting "important" things, so he had to run back to the house and then run to catch up. Important things, like the black cowboy hat he bought at the Dallas-Fort Worth airport, and his bucket of junk food and duct tape.

"You never know when that old gator will surface again," he said with a grin.

When we finally arrived at our destination—which was only about a hundred yards from Mamaw and Papaw's front porch—we spread the red-and-white checkered blankets out on the ground and plunked the baskets down.

Zeke, our director, seemed extra happy to finally get there.

It's not easy to move twenty-eight or so Carroways, even if it is only a hundred yards.

"Okay, Carroways, we'll start with a prayer and the meal, and then we'll film Papaw and the men doin' a little fishin' with the kids. How does that sound?"

"It sounds great if you give us time to eat," I said. "I can't sit still and do boring fishing if my stomach's growling."

No matter how hard I try, I can't get used to the *fishing* part of fishing. And I really don't like the baiting and the unhooking either. For that matter, the gutting and the cooking aren't my favorite. And I only like to eat *some* kinds of fish. So, I guess fishing is pretty much a bust for me.

"Ruby and I want to fish too," my Aunt Janie said.

"Did you bring poles?" Zeke asked.

Aunt Janie shook her head.

Zeke sighed. "Hannah, can you run back up to the house . . ."

"Sure, Zeke. I will return to the house for the SEVENTH time." Hannah, who is our wardrobe manager—and also manages equipment, our food, and sometimes, our preteen attitudes—pushed her hand through her short and sassy red hair. "Good thing I wore my hiking boots today."

She started back, but then turned to scowl at all of us. "Please, *don't* wait for me."

Zeke chuckled. "Hannah hates TV picnics."

The film crew moved in, and Zeke worked with them to position us for the best lighting.

"I want to sit next to Hunter!" My six-year-old cousin Chase, Lola and Ruby's little brother, scooted over and shoved himself between me and Hunter.

"That's just because his bucket is always filled with cookies," I said, and I reached in the bucket, pulled out a cookie, and popped it in my mouth.

"Allie," Mom called from the next blanket over, where she sat with my dad and my aunts and uncles. "Show some discipline."

I chomped and tried not to laugh. "Sorry, Mom. It's hard for us 'bayou people'."

"Bayou people?"

I was about to explain when I was rudely interrupted by a loud boat. It was chugging and sputtering toward us on the river. A horrible sound.

But the sight of the thing was even *more* horrible.

It was a Doonsberry boat. Complete with Doonsberrys on board!

Another boat, containing a film crew, floated next to what appeared to be the broken one that Mr. Doonsberry, Parker, and Madison were riding in.

Mr. Doonsberry cut the engine. "I'm bringing her up over here, Ron!" He waved an arm and pointed toward our family's private boat launch.

"Seems we got a party goin' on," my Papaw Ray said, and he rose from his picnic blanket, moaned and stretched a little, and walked toward the boat parade.

My mom and dad followed. Mamaw Kat stayed right where she was.

"Is that Andy Doonsberry? Hold on to your blankets kids, he may swipe 'em up and make boat canopies out of 'em."

She yelled it loud enough for Mr. Doonsberry to hear, and he laughed out loud and put his hand up above his eyes to shade the sun. The boat floated forward with the river current just a bit—enough to bring it up next to the dock so the Doonsberrys could step out—and onto Carroway private property.

Mr. Doonsberry walked past everyone, over to Mamaw, and gave her a big hug.

"Now, Kat, are you going to hold me accountable for something I did when I was just a little boy?"

Mamaw hugged him back but then pushed him playfully away. "Did you ask Jesus to forgive your sins yet?"

Mr. Doonsberry nodded. "Yes, ma'am. I've been a Christian for three years. It took a while, but one day I remembered all the things you used to try to teach me, and I finally let the Lord have my heart."

Mamaw shook her head. "Well, that's a relief. Welcome home, Andy."

Mr. Doonsberry grinned. "Thanks, Kat."

Most of us were up off our blankets now. The little kids ran in circles, chasing each other, my preteen girl cousins chatted in a circle while munching on some of Hunter's cookies, and Hunter took off to talk to Parker, who hung back near the disabled boat.

I stood alone, with my eye on Madison. She walked slowly over to the cousin circle, so I edged my way over there too.

My cousins parted to make room for Madison, and then me. Madison's eyes glued on Lola, and she scanned her from head to toe.

"I love your outfit," Madison said.

Lola smiled. "Thanks. I just threw a few things together."

"Can you come to my party?"

It was an awkward moment, with all of us "non-invites" standing around.

Lola's eyes darted over to meet mine. I gave her a tiny shrug and a half-grin.

She hesitated, looked down at the ground, and then over toward Hunter. She cleared her throat.

"Um . . . sure. I can come."

Madison's face lit up and she stepped back from the circle.

"Oh, I'm so honored, Lola! You're going to love all my friends. And, FYI, I *love* your necklace." Madison giggled. "Just a little hint for when you're shopping for my gift."

"So, you're Andrew's beautiful daughter." Mamaw pushed her way into our circle, right next to Madison. "I'm Mamaw Kat." Mamaw grinned and looked Madison right in the eyes. Madison turned away.

"I can't believe my dad used to live way out here," Madison said, as she gestured toward the buildings that make up Mamaw and Papaw's property. "Everything near the river seems so . . . run down."

Oh no, you did not just rudely turn your back and then say that to Mamaw.

Mamaw nodded and waved her hand in the air. "Oh, honey, you should have seen it before we did the extreme makeover!"

My cousins laughed, but I steamed on the inside. How dare she come chugging up here in her broken-down boat and insult my family!

"WHAT is going on here? I just go for a couple of poles and the whole day falls apart?" Hannah had made her way back from the house with some pink fishing poles.

She turned to Madison. "Hey, Red. Where'd *you* come from?"

Madison turned toward Hannah and held out her hand. "My name's Madison Doonsberry. I floated in on that boat over there. Maybe you've heard of my dad? Andrew Doonsberry? Star of *Lunker Law*?"

Hannah transferred the poles to her left hand and reached out to shake Madison's.

"Oh, so *you're* the rivals! I guess I'm supposed to hate your guts, but the show's hilarious! Hey—do you think we can catch a lunker on these girly poles?"

"Lunker" is a term fishermen use to describe a big fish.

No—a huge fish. The kind I hope I never catch when I'm forced to hold a fishing pole.

Madison put her hands on both cheeks. "I'm sorry to say this but . . ." she leaned forward and whispered, "I hate fishing."

Oh. We have something in common.

"But, you could ask my dad. He's the best fisherman around, and if you have any questions about the law, he can answer those too. He's a brilliant attorney. He knows much more than just those stupid Louisiana laws."

I watched Mamaw's eyebrows shoot up, and I wanted her to say something to defend our home state. Instead, she offered up some of her famous Louisiana hospitality.

"Madison, are you hungry? We have baskets filled with tasty food over here on the blankets." Mamaw gestured to where our family had been sitting.

Madison grimaced and held a hand out. "No, thank you. I wouldn't want to impose."

Ummm, yeah. Too late.

"Plus, I'm sure Daddy and the crew will have the boat going real soon." She put her hand to her throat and glanced over at the team that hovered around the disabled watercraft.

"Well, the boat's dead." My dad came over to give us that horrible news. "I'm goin' into town to get some parts. I told everyone they could hang out here. We got enough food, right Kat?"

Mamaw smiled big. "We sure do. But let's all head up to the house and eat there, what do you say? We can sit at real tables and then I can whip up somethin' even more spectacular."

I'm pretty sure I turned white, because I felt dizzy. I did *not* want Mad-girl in my grandparents' house.

She apparently didn't want to go either. She rushed over to her dad, and said something, her hands flailing in the air. Mr. Doonsberry pulled her aside, leaned over to look her in the

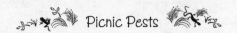

eyes, and waggled his finger in her face. Madison kicked the ground, and dust rose in a cloud which floated in my direction. Then she turned and stomped up toward the house.

My cousins and the rest of the family followed. I hung back, considering whether I should spend the rest of the afternoon out on the porch swing.

Mamaw came up behind me and spoke softly into my ear. "Allie-girl, you better start prayin' for that girl, but keep your eyes wide open. She's got a chip on her shoulder the size of Louisiana."

CHAPTER 5

Speech Impediment

I usually don't get nervous speaking in front of people. But right before going up to give my Student Project Manager campaign speech at school on Monday, I broke out in a sweat, my palms got all clammy, and my hands shook.

Maybe because at that moment, Miss Lewis walked in the room, with new student Madison Doonsberry at her side. Mad-girl smirked up at me, and I waved a slimy hand back at her.

This was no time to make anyone madder. I had a lot riding on this speech. So, why, oh why, had I thought it was a good idea to involve the dysfunctional Carroway dogs?

My cousins sat in the front row—their dogs laying down by their feet—except for T-Rex, who lay on his back while Hunter rubbed his belly and gave him doggy treats.

Hazel Mae began the fiasco by sneezing—like fifteen times. I think she fakes allergies for attention. So I had to take her up to the podium with me right from the start.

"Good morning, Ouachita Eagles." My voice wobbled, so I cleared my throat, and Hazel Mae sneezed again. The whole room erupted in laughter. The only thing I could think of to do was take a tissue out of my pants pocket and wipe her nose.

More laughter.

I continued. "One of the things I love best about Ouachita Middle School is the compassion the student body shows for our community. The end-of-the-year fundraiser has helped many people, and this year will be the best yet."

I looked down and stroked Hazel Mae's fluffy fur.

"How many of you own a dog?" I asked, and scanned the crowd as most everyone raised their hands. I glanced over at Madison. She kept her arms crossed in front of her body, and her nose pointed up in the air. She leaned her head over toward Miss Lewis to say something. Why wasn't she sitting with the rest of her class?

I felt sweat trickle down my back and into the waistband of my pants. This was not going well.

"Most of you know my cousins, Kendall, Hunter, Lola, and Ruby. We all have amazing dogs, which you may have seen on our show, *Carried Away with the Carroways*."

I noticed Madison rolling her eyes.

Quit looking at her! I scolded myself.

"But did you know that *all* of our dogs came from the West Monroe Animal Shelter?"

Random students shook their heads.

"The West Monroe Animal Shelter is currently home to thirty-seven dogs in need of families. The director, Mr. John Felix, and his staff, make an effort to get to know all of these animals personally, so that when your family comes looking for a dog, they can suggest one that will be a perfect match."

The dogs in front were getting bored by my speech. T-Rex barked a couple of times, and it appeared that Hunter had run out of treats.

I had to jump straight to the trick so I could get them out of there.

"I'd like you to meet—up close and personal—the Carroway dogs!"

One by one I introduced them. They looked so cool in the camo bandannas that Lola made for them. T-Rex got the most applause. He seemed to love the attention. He stood up on his back legs, and, for a second—before he lost his balance—it looked like he waved to the crowd.

I glanced over at Hunter, his eyes wide in reaction to this new trick.

I turned to the crowd. "Every dog deserves to have a loving family. And while a dog is waiting, it also deserves to have a home that is in good shape. The West Monroe Animal Shelter needs our help to improve and upgrade their facilities for our future dog family members. I would like to propose that as the end-of-the-year project, we hold a carnival, as usual, but we'll call it a Canine Carnival, because all the proceeds will go to the West Monroe Animal Shelter."

Applause erupted from the crowd. Our dogs yelped along. Madison's arms relaxed, and hung by her sides, but she didn't clap. And her face seemed to turn from mad to . . . well, sad, I think.

"And that's not all," I continued. "In addition, we'll give all you dog owners a chance to participate in a Spectacular Dog Trick competition. We'll bring in some top dog-trainers to show you how to teach your dogs tricks like this . . ."

On cue, Hunter handed T-Rex's leash off to Kendall, and he ran to the side of the room to drag over the mini-tramp. Then he retrieved the hula hoop.

I breathed in deep and then made the announcement, sounding very much like a ringmaster at the circus.

"Ladies and gentlemen, boys and girls, the Carroway cousins and their dogs bring you . . . The Carroway Catapult!"

I closed my eyes briefly and prayed that it wouldn't go down in history as the Carroway Catastrophe.

CHAPTER 6

Flips and Flops

The practice the other day at Ruby and Lola's had paid off. Max and Monet began the trick by running around the perimeter of the room, and performing perfect jumps through the hoop. Kids gasped and clapped. Then Ellie pranced around, and in her ladylike way, approached the trampoline, tested it with her paw, then hopped up. She bounced five times—the kids counted each one—and then she rolled beautifully through the hoop. Hazel Mae sneezed a couple of times, but then jumped out of my arms and tore around the room. She leaped, barely touching the mini-tramp, and then flew through the hoop. She forgot to flip or roll in the air, but made up for it when she landed, rolling over and over until she was laying at my feet, sneezing again. I picked her up and wiped her nose.

Out of the corner of my eye, I think I saw Madison grin a little.

T-Rex provided the grand finale. He was a wildcard, since even after all our practice the other day, all he managed to do was jump through the hoop from the ground. I was tempted to cut him completely out of the act, but Hunter had begged profusely.

"I promise the T won't disappoint," he said.

So I kept him in. And I was about to find out if that was a mistake.

Hunter pulled a few surprise treats out of his back pocket. He kneeled and hugged T-Rex, roughing his neck up.

"Okay, boy, show them what you can do!" Hunter pointed toward the back of the room, and T-Rex ran through the rows of kids, getting petted along the way. Chants began, row by row. "T-Rex! T-Rex! T-Rex!"

Soon he emerged from the crowd and skittered around to the side of the room. At one point, he stopped, lifted his front foot and brushed it back along the ground, like a bull approaching a bull fighter.

"T-Rex! T-Rex! T-Rex!"

Then T-Rex bolted forward, toward the mini-tramp. I said another prayer, this one so that we wouldn't need to call the doggy ambulance in a minute.

T-Rex ran toward the mini-tramp, and I started to put my hands up to cover my eyes. But then, right when he should have jumped up on the tramp, he stopped. The whole room became still.

And T-Rex squatted and crawled *under* the trampoline.

It was like a game of Doggy-Limbo!

Eventually, T-Rex emerged from under the trampoline. Hunter held up the hula hoop, and T-Rex stepped through to a standing ovation from all the students at Ouachita Middle School.

Madison had already been standing, so it was hard to tell if she appreciated the trick or not.

There wasn't much else for me to say, except, "If you vote for me for Student Project Manager, all the dogs of West Monroe will benefit, and that will definitely add more joy to our beautiful town. Thank you."

I was the last person to give my speech, so as soon as I finished, the students began to file out of the multipurpose room, class by class. My two competitors, Ronnie Alexander and Samara James, both came over to shake my hand and congratulate me.

"It's not even gonna be close," Ronnie said. "I think I'll even vote for you."

Samara, who I've known since kindergarten, gave me a side hug. "Can I serve on the committee? I'm really good at decorations—and I have three dogs!"

I smiled, though I felt a little embarrassed. "The vote isn't in yet, but if I win, I'd love to have you both on my committee. We'll need everyone's talent to make this the best year-end project ever."

Ronnie and Samara left the podium. The next people to greet me were the students in my class. Mrs. Mellon was at the front of the line.

"That was exceptional, Allie. Every year I'm amazed at what our students come up with for project ideas."

Right behind Mrs. Mellon was Parker Doonsberry. Parker never crosses his arms or scowls. He's a quiet one, and Kendall says the expressions he makes and the reflections from his dark green eyes make you wonder what enchanting thoughts he is having at any given moment.

I tilted my head and smiled. "Welcome to OMS, Parker."

Parker brushed his wavy strawberry blonde bangs to the side of his face.

"Thanks. This is a nice school. And, hey—your idea sounds great."

"Thanks."

The kids in my class began to file out, but Parker stayed for a minute, watching the door until every kid was gone. Soon, just he and I stood there alone in the multipurpose room.

"Is everything okay?" I asked.

Parker fidgeted.

"Yeah. It's just, I wanted you to know something." He turned his head, left, then right.

"O . . . kay."

I waited.

He finally spit it out. "Madison, uh . . . you know my sister?"

I nodded.

Yeah. Mad-girl.

"Well, she's been having a really bad year."

I know. The divorce. The move. I suppose that would be hard.

Parker took a deep breath and blew it out. "And, right before we left Florida, her golden retriever, Millie, who she's had all her life, got really sick."

Gulp.

"And we had to put her down."

My mouth went dry. I pulled Hazel Mae in a little closer.

"Don't tell Madison I told you, okay?"

"Okay."

Parker reached out to pet Hazel Mae for a second, then he turned and ran out the door.

CHAPTER 7

Miss Lewis

There's never been a teacher that scared me quite like Miss Lewis. She's barely five feet tall, and I'm pretty sure she only weighs a hundred pounds. Rumors have it that she was an army boot camp sergeant, but she was discharged because she was sending too many troops to the hospital before they even made it to combat.

My older brother Cody had the bad luck of being in Miss Lewis's class when he was in eighth grade. He spent most of the year in detention, and *he* was a straight-A student! Okay, maybe he played practical jokes from time to time, but Cody says that's what kept the class sane.

"Today's the day I will make her smile," Cody used to say when he left in the morning.

That was five years ago, and I'm pretty sure Miss Lewis hasn't smiled yet. This year, Lola and Hunter are in her class. Now, if Hunter can't make that lady smile, it's *impossible* for anyone to do it.

But here we were in late March, and nothing yet.

"She grins with her eyes," Hunter claims, but I hadn't seen it.

"Miss Carroway, don't you have a classroom to get to instead gawking over that boy?" Miss Lewis had appeared out of nowhere, and now stood by the podium where I was holding Hazel Mae.

"Yes, ma'am. I'm headed there right now."

"Well, good. I'd hate to think you would waste good educational time daydreaming after a flirt session."

"No, ma'am. I'm sorry, ma'am."

And I *wasn't flirting*!

Miss Lewis stood in front of me, in between the podium and the door. I couldn't decide which way to step around her. What if she stepped in the same direction as me, and we bumped into each other? Would she make me drop down and give her twenty push-ups?

Hazel Mae sneezed.

Miss Lewis kept her stern face, but reached over to pet Hazel Mae. "Poor baby. You sound like you need a decongestant."

Miss Lewis stepped back. "Good speech, Carroway. I wish you the best in the election."

I tried to keep my jaw from hitting the floor. Had that been a compliment?

"Um . . . thank you, ma'am."

Miss Lewis pointed her index finger in the air.

"'Um' is not a word. Remember that. Stammering reveals lack of confidence, and if you are going to be a leader, you *must* be confident."

Miss Lewis did an about-face before she marched over to the door of the multipurpose room.

Madison Doonsberry was waiting for her there, writing on a clipboard. When Miss Lewis reached her, she handed her the clipboard, and they marched out together.

A screechy voice crackled over the loudspeaker, interrupting my thoughts. It was Jared Strickland, our student body president.

"The election for Student Project Manager will take place *today only* during lunch. Bring your school ID to the front table in the quad to cast your vote. The winner will be announced before the closing bell today. Thank you, and good luck to all of our outstanding candidates."

"Yeah, let's hope we win," I said to Hazel Mae, and walked back to my homeroom class.

When I came through the door, all heads turned my way, and a smattering of applause started from the back of the class and traveled forward. A beaming Mrs. Mellon sat in front on a stool with a literature textbook balanced open on her lap, her dark-brown hair pulled back in a stylish ponytail. She had started wearing the cutest maternity clothes just a couple of weeks ago, and the glow on her face complemented the orange-red poppy necklace that matched her top.

"Great job on your speech, Allie. If you end up winning the position, I hope I'll have the stamina to keep up with your plan."

She placed her hand on her little tiny baby bump and sighed a little.

"I'm going to miss working here next school year."

Mrs. Mellon's baby was due at the beginning of August. All the seventh-graders had been excited about that—my cousin Ruby especially—assuming Mrs. Mellon would be able to have the baby during summer vacation and then return to school in the fall. But during a lunch break last week, Mrs. Mellon broke the bad news.

"I'm taking a leave of absence, and I'm not sure when I'll be back. I never thought I would be able to have kids, and I may never have another—so I'm going to stay home and savor every minute with my little girl."

The sparkle in her eyes had been so beautiful that no one had the heart to challenge her decision, or even to express frustration. The school would get a good teacher to fill her position, but *no one* could replace someone as special as Mrs. Mellon.

"Mrs. Mellon, may I be excused for a minute? My mom's coming to pick up my dog."

Mrs. Mellon smiled.

"Of course. Come on back as soon as you can. We're reviewing for the lit test tomorrow."

I hurried out the door, through the quad, and spotted our family's white SUV in the parking lot—my dependable mom in the driver's seat. She opened her door and stepped out to give me a hug.

"How did the speech go?"

I reached in the driver side and let Hazel Mae loose in the front seat. Then I brushed her little white hairs off my navy-blue T-shirt.

"It went better than expected, and T-Rex stole the show at the end by doing a limbo under the mini-tramp."

Mom laughed. "Leave it to Hunter to come up with something clever."

"Yeah. And I think the students all love the idea. The votes aren't in yet, but I have a really good feeling about it."

Mom nodded. "Oh, I'm sure you'll be elected. You're determined, a great leader, and everyone around here loves you."

"Well, *most* people do. Miss Lewis got mad at me for using the word, 'um,' and Madison Doonsberry showed up today and glared at me during the whole assembly."

"Okay, so that's two people who may not be your fans. Madison just needs time to get to know you, and Miss Lewis is not really a fan of anyone. I'm proud of you for taking on such a huge project."

I smiled. "It's going to be awesome. Between me and Mrs. Mellon—this is going to be the best year-end project in the school's history."

CHAPTER 8

Complications

Mom and I talked for a few more minutes, which helped calm me down after my stressful speech.

"Okay, I guess I better get back to class," I said, and Mom jumped back in the SUV with Hazel Mae.

"See you this afternoon." She waved at me through the open driver's side window, began to back up, but didn't get far before she had to stop and pull back in.

Sirens blared as a fire truck and ambulance entered the circular driveway in front of the school.

Mr. Langley, our principal who happens to be 6' 8" and has the longest legs I've ever seen, ran out of the administration office and reached the ambulance in about six steps.

He waited for the EMTs to drag out a gurney, and then he pointed them in the direction they needed to go.

"It's this way," Mr. Langley said. "Room 217."

I gasped. "That's my class!"

Mom jumped out of the SUV and ran with me in the direction of the classroom.

About the time we got to the door, kids began to pile out, Kendall and Parker leading the way.

Kendall's eyes were wide as she pulled me to the middle of the quad where the class was gathering. "It's Mrs. Mellon! She was reading to us, and then she stopped, grabbed her stomach, and almost fell off the stool. Parker ran up to help, and she just crumpled on the floor. Allie, do you think something's wrong with the baby?"

My heart pounded as I locked my eyes on the open door of the classroom.

"We need to pray for her."

"Right now?"

"Yes! Help me gather some kids."

"Allie, this is a public school. We'll get in trouble if we pray."

"I don't care."

I spoke to the waiting crowd of kids.

"People, we're forming a circle over here to pray for Mrs. Mellon. You can join us if you want."

About half the class came over and tried to form a circle, but it ended up looking more like a figure eight. Kendall ended up on my left, and Parker was on my right. Kendall grabbed my hand, and the rest of the kids grabbed hands too. I didn't know if I should grab Parker's hand or not. I didn't have to think long, because Parker reached over, grabbed mine, and began to pray:

"Dear Jesus, please be with Mrs. Mellon and her baby right now. Help them to be okay. Help the doctors know what to do."

There was a silence. Parker had said it all in such a simple way. I knew I should add something, but my brain was fuzzy and my hands were starting to shake. I felt a warm hand on my shoulder and then heard Mom finish up the prayer for us.

"Thank you, Lord, that you know exactly what is going on right now with Mrs. Mellon. Give her peace and comfort. We trust you and love you. Amen."

Mom squeezed my shoulder, and I opened my eyes. I immediately dropped Parker's hand, and then gave Kendall a hug.

"I hope she's gonna be okay," Kendall said.

"I'm sure she will be."

I heard squeaking wheels behind me, so I turned to watch

as the EMTs rolled Mrs. Mellon out. She was laying down, had a blanket pulled up to her chest, her right arm extended outside the blanket with an IV stuck in it. EMT number one held a bag, while number two wheeled the gurney. Mr. Langley walked awkwardly next to them, trying to bend down to talk to Mrs. Mellon. I moved as close as I could to hear what he was saying.

"I called your husband, and he's going to meet us at the hospital. You're going to be okay, Christie."

Mrs. Mellon didn't say anything, but she did turn her head to look at us kids.

"We're praying for you!" I yelled, and I saw her nod and grin just a little before EMT number two wheeled the gurney into the parking lot. We all just stood there and stared as they opened the back of the ambulance, loaded Mrs. Mellon in, and took off, siren blaring.

Our school secretary, Mrs. West, came out to the quad to meet Mr. Langley.

"Daniel, I found a sub, but he can't get here until after lunch."

Mr. Langley nodded. "That's fine, Sabrina. Let's just have them go to Megan's class for right now, and after I get back from the hospital I'll go get them."

This morning was just getting worse. "Megan" was none other than Miss Lewis!

I turned to my mom.

"Can you take me out of school so we can go check on Mrs. Mellon in the hospital?"

Mom frowned.

"No! You need to be in school."

I gave her my very best boo-boo face.

"Pleeeeease?"

"NO."

Mom *never* falls for the boo-boo face.

"Okay, kids." Mr. Langley gestured toward a classroom door in the far corner of the quad. "Go on over to room 220. I'm going to the hospital, but then I'll be over to get you."

Everyone knew the meaning of this, so everyone *trudged* to the classroom in the corner. We had been the lucky ones at the beginning of the year—being assigned to Mrs. Mellon's class instead of Miss Lewis's.

But now our luck had run out.

"I think we need to pray again," Kendall said.

I chuckled.

"And make sure we don't say, 'um'."

When our group entered the classroom, the murmuring began.

"What happened?" "Why are they here?" "Is Mrs. Mellon okay?" were some of the statements swirling around the room. One of our custodians, Mr. Jarvis, brought a rolling cart with some folding chairs for us to sit in at the back and sides of the room.

"What about the year-end project?" Samara—who was a student in Miss Lewis's class—asked. "We need Mrs. Mellon for that."

My stomach jumped up into my throat.

Surely she'll be back in a couple of days, right? Maybe she's dehydrated or having morning sickness, like she did after Christmas break. Right?

Miss Lewis frowned and snapped her fingers.

"Okay, now, let's regain our concentration. It doesn't matter how many students they shove in here, you still have a math test this afternoon."

46

Miss Lewis's class directed their attention back to their math books, and the rest of us just stared into space. Hunter turned his head for a moment to look at me with his questioning eyes. He raised a palm up in the air.

I shrugged, and mouthed, "I don't know."

And then someone nudged me from behind and handed me a note.

A note? Seriously, people? Do you know whose classroom you're in?

My hands shook as I pulled the note over on my lap. I clamped it between my knees while I scanned the room for Miss Lewis's location.

She was helping a student at her desk. Wow, that kid was brave to approach.

I slowly released the note from my legs and tried not to make any noise as I unfolded it.

The words were scrawled in green ink:

> *Madi D is upset that she didn't get a chance to run for SPM.*

"Madi D" had just been admitted to our school a couple of hours ago. How could she be mad already and have everyone know about it?

I glanced over to where Madison was sitting—in the front row just diagonal from Miss Lewis's desk.

Because she's a Mad-girl, that's why.

I looked back to see who had handed me the note, but no eyes met mine. Instead, everyone's eyes were glued on something straight ahead.

I turned. Miss Lewis had left her seat at her desk and was now standing in front of me.

"Something you'd like to share with the class, Carroway?"

Gulp.

"No, ma'am."

Miss Lewis reached out with her open hand, and I had no choice but to give up the note. She opened it and read it to herself. Then she turned her head to look over to where Madison was sitting, reading a book.

Miss Lewis looked back at me, her lips pressed together.

I tried to keep eye contact, but finally had to drop my head. Miss Lewis stares are intense.

"Thank you, Miss Carroway. I will take this under advisement."

And then she walked away.

My deodorant failed me at that moment. Too much excitement, drama, chills, and thrills for one morning. Thirty minutes later, Mr. Langley arrived to save the day.

He walked up to the front of the class, and wiped the back of his hand across his forehead.

"I have an update on Mrs. Mellon. As you know, she's pregnant, and well, she's gone into labor. Please keep her and the baby in your thoughts and prayers."

Labor? But she's not even five months pregnant!

Mr. Langley continued.

"Mrs. Mellon's class, can you please line up at the door? We'll be returning to room 217 now."

The buzz began again, with comments like "Is she having the baby today?" "Can they stop the labor?" and "Who's gonna be our sub?"

My headache began at that moment. It was a dull ache, at the base of my skull.

It would last for the next two months.

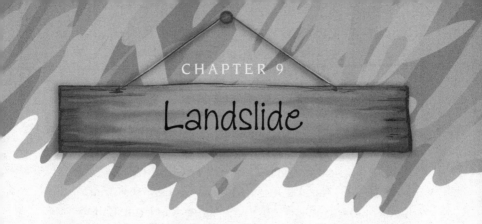

CHAPTER 9

Landslide

Mr. Langley did his best to entertain us for the next two hours. He finished reading the short story Mrs. Mellon had been reading when she fell off her stool, then he performed some of his famous magic tricks, and showed a National Geographic movie about alligators.

The narrator's monotone voice droned on . . .

Alligators are the bullies of the bayou. Their approach,
slow and crafty, their attack swift and deadly. Many
naïve victims have been trapped in the mighty jaws and
have been dragged to the depths, never to be seen again.
Wise visitors to the bayou who wish to survive will keep
their eyes wide open whenever they are in gator territory.

Goosebumps rose on my arms and spread to my torso as I remembered Mamaw's warning about Madison: *Pray, but keep your eyes wide open. That girl's got a chip on her shoulder the size of Louisiana.*

I shifted in my chair and glanced up at the wall clock. Three minutes until lunch, and the election for Student Project Manager.

And for some reason, I was nervous.

But not that I would lose. That I might win.

The bell rang for lunch. I reached for my backpack and shot out the door, eager to join Kendall, Ruby, Lola, and Hunter at our usual round table in the middle of the covered quad, located right outside our classroom doors.

Jared Strickland and our Student Body Vice-President, Paige Wright, sat at a rectangular table near the front of the quad, ready to check off names and hand out ballots. My cousins and I stared at their backs as we dug into our lunch sacks.

"I think everyone in the school is going to vote for you," Hunter said. "Did you see how they clapped for T-Rex?"

"Your speech was awesome, Allie." Lola opened her pink paisley backpack—that happened to match her scarf—and pulled out a fruit cup. "I'm sure we'll raise a record amount of money for the animal shelter."

I unwrapped my sandwich, but couldn't take even one bite.

"Allie, is something wrong?" Ruby, who was sitting next to me, reached over and put her hand on my wrist. "You look a little pale."

My cousins are always checking my face shade. When my allergies attack, I tend to lose color from my cheeks, and sometimes my freckles turn from light brown to pale peach in a matter of seconds.

I tried to take a deep breath, but it was difficult. I ran through the possible reasons why in my head:

Did you just eat a peanut? No.

Are you sitting in a moldy swamp? No.

I checked my surroundings, but nothing appeared to be a threat. There were just a bunch of middle-school kids eating, goofing around, laughing, and talking. But . . . wait a minute. There was *one* cause for alarm.

Madison Doonsberry sat next to her brother and some of

the kids in Miss Lewis's class, just two tables away. And she was glaring at me.

With the heavy feeling still in my chest, I stood and walked over to the Mad-girl. Might as well meet the problem head on.

"Hey, Madison," I sort of wheezed that out. "Welcome to OMS."

Madison didn't look up, but instead focused on her school lunch and stirred her fish stick around in tartar sauce.

"Thanks." She grinned at the people at her table. "Are you here to ask for my vote?"

She finally looked up at me, and flipped her hair behind her shoulder.

"No. I came over to . . . ."

"Because I already decided that I'm voting for you."

"Huh?"

I'm *sure* my freckles turned peach at that moment.

"I said, I'm *voting* for you. I mean, I know you can't control your *own* dog, but it's a great idea to have a dog show. I'm sure if I ask my daddy he'll be willing to contribute lots of time and money to help make it a success."

"Did you know Madison's dad is the guy on *Lunker Law*?" Joey Sanger, another kid I've known since kindergarten, sat next to Parker, looking star-struck.

Madison cocked her head. "Well, he's Parker's daddy too."

"I *love* that show!" Kyra Barker, one of my favorite friends from the cheer squad, sat next to Madison with stars in her eyes too. Great.

Kyra shrugged. "I just love fishing." She must have seen my shocked expression, because she followed her comment up with, "But don't worry, Allie, my family records your show and we still watch it together if we have time."

If we have time.

"Madison," Joey said, "do you think you could get your dad to bring his cool fishing boat with all the gadgets to the carnival and take pictures with us kids?"

Madison was all charm now. "Oh, yes, I know he'll come. Plus, I have some other ideas to bring in some money . . ."

It sounded to me like Madison was the one campaigning.

"Well, let's go vote, shall we?" Madison rose, and stepped backwards over the bench to stand next to me. Then she called out to the crowd.

"Allie Carroway for Student Project Manager! A vote for Allie is a vote for all the adorable dogs of West Monroe."

At her request, several kids moved from their lunch tables toward the ballot box. Samara James walked past me and patted me on the shoulder. A bunch of my friends gathered around Madison, who was in the middle of the line that was now forming by the voting table. Soon, the only kids still eating were my cousins at the middle table, and Parker Doonsberry, who I now felt I should talk to.

I sat down across the round table from where he was munching on a pickle.

"So, Parker, how's your day going? In case you're wondering, we don't usually have an assembly, a visit from emergency services, spontaneous prayer on the quad, and an election all in one day."

Parker grinned, took a napkin, and wiped pickle juice from his chin. "It's been good so far, but I hope Mrs. Mellon's okay."

That reminded me that Parker had been the one to pray earlier.

"Hey, Parker." I cleared my throat. "Are you a Christian?"

Parker nodded. "Not for very long though. My dad started taking us to church a couple of years ago. A few months later I accepted Jesus as my savior."

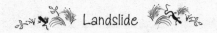

There was an awkward silence. I really, really, really wanted to ask if Madison had done the same thing.

I glanced over to the voting line. Madison was up to bat, and she took a pen, marked a paper, folded it, and looked up to meet my glance. She nodded, smiled (or maybe it was a smirk), and she dropped it in the box.

"Hmmmm, that's weird." I meant to just *think* that, but instead it came out so Parker could hear.

"I agree," he said. And then he packed up his things and went to go join the line.

The afternoon dragged on for me, even though I had choir after lunch, and then when I returned to homeroom for math, one of my favorite subs, Mr. Vicker, was there. He's a black belt in Tae Kwan Do, but you would never know by his calm demeanor. Last time he came, he brought some boards, and when we became frustrated with a math problem, he showed us how to yell and kick and break the boards in half. Students refer to him as Vicker the Kicker.

"I'm sorry to hear about your teacher," Mr. Vicker said. "Since it's been a rough day for everyone, I'm going to let you have free time today—just read or work on homework quietly at your desks."

Most of the class seemed relieved by that, but I needed something to occupy my mind so I could stop trying to figure out Madison Doonsberry and her sneaky ways. I pulled out my Bible and tried to read a whole chapter of Psalms, but I just kept reading the same line over and over:

Don't worry about the wicked, or envy those who do

wrong. For like grass, they will soon fade away. Like spring flowers they soon wither.

PSALM 37:1 (NLT)

Reading *that* made me worry more! Was Madison trying to do *me* wrong? And if so, why? What did I ever do to *her* (besides lose track of Hazel Mae a couple of times)?

Finally, the clock reached 3:15, and a crackly Jared voice came over the loudspeaker. "Fellow OMS students, we have the results of today's election . . ."

The headache at the base of my neck pounded, my chest felt like a brick lay on it, and my fingers became all tingly.

Really? I'm going to have an asthma attack right now?

I opened my backpack and pulled out my little pink wrist pack that holds my Epi-pen and inhaler. I pulled off the cap, blew out, and then put the inhaler to my mouth.

Jared continued, "We'd like to thank all our candidates for putting themselves out there and sharing some great ideas. Those who were not elected are automatically appointed to the steering committee, and we are confident that all who serve will do a great job."

I pushed the button on the inhaler and I breathed in, the propellant carrying the much-needed medicine to my airways.

"And now for our winner . . ."

I took another puff.

"By the way, this year's Student Project Manager won by a landslide, capturing the heart of this school with her idea. If you see her, please congratulate our new Student Project Manager—Allie Carroway!"

My class applauded as I took another puff.

The last time I took three puffs on my inhaler was . . . never.

CHAPTER 10

And Now ... the Bad News

I could hear clapping and whistling coming from other class-rooms through our thin walls.

"Congratulations, Allie," Mr. Vicker said. "I would be happy to contribute monetarily to the event, and I would love to bring my Tae Kwan Do students to do a demonstration if you would like."

"Thank you, sir."

I sat up straight and tried to force air down my throat by yawning. Three minutes till the bell rang. Hopefully a change of atmosphere would wake my lungs up.

But Jared wasn't done with his announcements.

"Allie Carroway, Ronnie Alexander, and Samara James, please meet in the library tomorrow at lunch for your first Canine Carnival Steering Committee meeting."

Then Jared cleared his throat. "And now, please listen carefully for an important message from Mr. Langley."

I held my breath.

"Good afternoon, students. Many of you know that Mrs. Mellon was taken by ambulance to the hospital this morning. I want to thank all the students and staff for their cooperation during that emergency. I am *always* proud of the way OMS Eagles handle challenges we face every day. I have an update for you . . ."

I blew out, and my neck began to sweat.

"Mrs. Mellon gave birth to a baby girl today at 2:41. As you know, she was not due to deliver until August, so this baby is a tiny preemie. Bethany Elaine Mellon weighed in at one pound, four ounces. She is in the Neonatal ICU ward at West Monroe Regional Hospital. Please keep little Bethany in your thoughts and prayers."

The room was dead still. Mr. Vicker rubbed the back of his neck, and it looked like he was trying to form words. The bell rang, but nobody moved.

"Is the baby gonna survive?" Kendall finally asked what we all wanted to know.

"I don't know," Mr. Vicker said. "But we have an outstanding medical staff at our hospital, and we have a great God, so there's all kinds of hope."

I flew to the door and was the first one out. Though my breathing was still labored, I ran as fast as I could to the large grassy area behind the school—the place where we usually hold the year-end carnival. I threw my backpack down and lay on my back. As soon as I did, dark clouds appeared out of nowhere, blocking the bright Louisiana sun.

Lord, what is going on? Why did Mrs. Mellon have her baby today? And how can a baby that tiny survive?

I cried a little bit. I had seen preemies in the NICU before—so helpless and attached to tons of tubes. I counted on my fingers how many months remained till August.

Bethany Mellon had been born about four-and-a-half months premature.

Raindrops began to fall on my face, and thunder roared in the distance.

And having a premature infant meant . . . no way Mrs. Mellon could be the faculty advisor for the Canine Carnival and Dog Show.

CHAPTER 11

Cousins to the Rescue

Allie! There you are!" Lola ran to where I was laying in the rain and got the knees of her stylish leggings wet when she kneeled to check on me. "Are you having an asthma attack?" She held one hand out to lift me up to a sitting position.

I grabbed my forehead. "I don't know. I'm short of breath, and the inhaler didn't work, even after three puffs."

"Why did you run all the way out here? You could have passed out and no one would have known!"

I rested my face in my hands. "I'm sorry. I'm just really upset about Mrs. Mellon's baby."

And what is going to happen with the project.

Lola sat down next to me. "We all are." We stayed there for a moment, getting watered by the warm sprinkles. "We'll just have to keep praying real hard. God will keep her safe." Lola put an arm around my shoulders.

"Hey—congratulations on winning the election. Our whole class seemed happy about it—even Madison."

"Thanks. It's going to be a lot of work, and now with Mrs. Mellon out . . ."

Lola gasped and put a hand to her mouth. "Oh, no, Allie! I hadn't even thought about that! What are you going to do?"

I stood and brushed the grass off my jeans. "I dunno. Resign? Is that an option? I mean, I've only officially been SPM for about ten minutes."

Lola picked up my backpack and handed it to me. "You

can't resign. Your idea is way too good. You should have heard everyone talking about their dogs as we were leaving today. They can't wait for them to learn new tricks."

Kendall, Hunter, and Ruby came running out to the grass to meet us.

"Oh, good, you found her!" Hunter put his hand out to catch some rain. "What are you doing out here? Are you okay?"

Lola answered for me. "She's fine. She's just having a little panic attack since Mrs. Mellon won't be helping with the school project."

"Panic?" I brushed her comment off with my hand. "No, it was asthma. And I'm better now."

"Allie, you haven't had an asthma attack since you moved out of your old house and we got rid of the moldy Diva." Kendall crossed her arms and raised an eyebrow. "I think Lola's right."

"I know I'd panic if I just got elected Student Project Manager." Ruby reached out and pulled a piece of grass out of my hair. "Don't worry, Allie, we'll all help you out. I can organize a gigantic bake sale."

"And I have an idea that will bring in tons of money," Hunter said. "I gotta talk to Mr. Dimple about it first, but soon I'll reveal my plan."

Mr. Dimple is the town inventor. If he got involved in the year-end project, we could be catapulting dogs to the moon and back.

"And I can line up some talent, so you have music goin' all day long," Kendall said.

"Would you like me to paint a mural?" Lola asked. "We can come up with a theme, and then we can gift it to the animal shelter to put up on one of the walls."

My shoulders began to relax as I heard all my cousins' ideas. We Carroways could practically pull this thing off by ourselves. I breathed in deep and smiled.

"Thanks, you guys. I feel a lot better now."

The sprinkles gave way to real rain, so we ran back to the safety of the covered quad area and sat down at our regular center table.

"Where's Aunt Kassie?" I plopped my backpack down and scanned the empty parking lot. My aunt—Hunter and Kendall's mom—was supposed to pick us up today, and she's always early.

Kendall checked her phone. "Uh-oh. Here's a text from Mom." She sighed and read out loud, "Got a flat. Be there soon."

"Well, I'm starving," Hunter said. "Anyone have any lunch left?"

I pulled my half-eaten sandwich out of my backpack. "Here you go. You need to stop growing. Good thing you always wear shorts, so you don't have to worry about flood pants."

Hunter took a huge bite and talked while he chewed. "Yeah, I know. I keep running into doorways and knocking over cups. I think my arms have grown two inches this spring, and I'm not used to it."

Ruby pulled some homemade kettle corn out of her backpack and poured some into each of our hands.

"You should make *this* at the carnival," I said. "People can't stop eating this stuff."

Ruby smiled. "Whatever you want, cousin."

Right then, the door of the administration office flew open, and out walked a very tall Mr. Langley, and a very short—but tough-looking—Miss Lewis.

Mr. Langley looked over at our table and then walked over with Miss Lewis.

"Did someone forget to pick up the famous Carroway cousins?"

Kendall held up her phone and pointed to it. "Flat tire. She's on her way."

Mr. Langley nodded. "Oh, well that's good. And this is fortuitous timing, since I wanted to talk to you anyway, Allie."

"You wanted to talk to me?" I said through my kettle-corn crunching.

"Yes. First, I'd like to congratulate you on being elected Student Project Manager—and by a landslide victory! That shows how much confidence all the kids in this school have in you."

"Thank you, sir. I feel privileged to serve."

And terrified.

Mr. Langley continued, "But I *was* a little worried when Christie—I mean Mrs. Mellon—went out today. I wasn't sure who we would replace her with for faculty advisor."

I swallowed hard and tried to put on a brave front. "I'm sure we'll find someone. If you want, I can talk to some teachers and see if anyone . . ."

Mr. Langley held his hand out to stop me. "Not necessary, because we've already had a volunteer."

"See, Allie?" Lola patted me on the back. "I told you everything would be okay."

Mr. Langley smiled. "Yes, it will be *more* than okay, and we won't lose any planning time at all, because Miss Lewis has volunteered to take over the project starting today."

My ears began to ring, but I'm not sure if it was because of my sudden, increased headache, or because the clouds burst open at that moment, sending a driving rain that pounded on the aluminum roof that covers the quad. It was too loud to hear words, and it was a good thing, because I don't think anyone knew what to say. Finally, the rain died down, and Miss Lewis spoke.

"I'm looking forward to the challenge, Carroway. Meet me in my classroom at 0600 tomorrow. We've got a boatload of planning to do before the steering committee meeting."

CHAPTER 12

Comedy Night

Aunt Kassie finally arrived to pick us up, but I hardly remember getting in her car. We stopped at Walmart on the way home, but I couldn't tell you what for. I don't remember the conversations between my cousins, and I would have forgotten to buckle my seatbelt after leaving Walmart if Lola hadn't reached for it and shoved the strap in my hand.

"Allie, everything's going to be okay. I've been in her class all year and look at me. I'm surviving."

I scanned Lola's face, and noticed that little eye twitch that she'd picked up over the last few months. She'd also taken up biting her pinkie fingernail.

"Remember, she grins with her eyes," Hunter said. "And, I actually saw her forehead relax when she said 0600. Next thing you know, one corner of her mouth will turn up. You'll see."

"0600." I tipped my head back on the headrest. "What time is that exactly?"

Aunt Kassie caught my eye from the rearview. "That's six o'clock in the morning. You may have to call a taxi."

"What could she possibly want me to do that early? School doesn't start until eight."

Kendall threw a hand up in the air. "Calisthenics? A little mile running? Who knows with Miss Lewis."

Aunt Kassie chuckled. "You kids exaggerate so much when it comes to that Miss Lewis."

Kendall jumped on that. "Oh, no, there's no exaggeration. She really is that horrible."

"Kendall . . ." Aunt Kassie turned around and gave Kendall the stink-eye.

"Ask Wesley, he'll tell you. He and Cody spent most of the year in detention."

Wesley is Kendall and Hunter's older brother, and he's a practical joker, just like Cody.

Hunter started laughing. "Did they really set off fireworks on their class fieldtrip to Black Bayou Lake?"

"No!" Aunt Kassie said. "It wasn't them."

"But Miss Lewis blamed 'em for it," Kendall said. "And they had to clean the school grounds every day after school for a month."

"And Miss Lewis hates Carroways because of that," I said.

"Hate is a strong word," Aunt Kassie said. "I prefer we don't use it from here on out."

"I'm a Carroway," Hunter said. "And she doesn't dislike me."

"Oh, yeah?" Kendall said. "What about that dinosaur essay you worked so hard on last month? You got, what? A D?"

"But it *was* really bad, Kendall. And she let me make improvements. She said that essay would never cut it in high school."

"Don't ya see, little brother? You're not *in* high school yet, so she's goin' overboard on ya. I'm glad I didn't end up in her class this year."

Aunt Kassie pulled the car into the driveway. Then she turned to talk to us.

"Okay, time out. You need to stop all this negative talk. Y'all are better than that. God loves Miss Lewis, so even if she isn't your favorite, you need to try to love her too. Love your enemies, remember?"

"Yes, ma'am," Ruby said. "We just need to pray for Allie not to have any more panic attacks."

Aunt Kassie raised her eyebrows. "Panic attacks? Allie, does your mom know about this?"

I shook my head. "I'm not having panic attacks. Just a really bad asthma attack today at the end of school."

"And her inhaler didn't help one bit."

Thanks a lot, Lola.

"Huh." Aunt Kassie gave me the once-over. Then she thought a minute, and grinned. "You know what I think we all need? We need a Carroway Comedy Night."

"Yeah!" Hunter pumped his fist and accidentally punched the ceiling of the car. "Ouch!" He grabbed his knuckles. "Long arms are gonna kill me."

"Can we do it tonight?" Ruby asked.

Aunt Kassie checked the time on her phone. "Sure! We were gonna grill some burgers anyway, so we'll just send out a text invite and see how many Carroways show up!"

"Can we invite Uncle Saul?" Hunter's eyes lit up. "He promised to do a karaoke duet with me on the next comedy night."

"Yes, we'll invite Uncle Saul." Aunt Kassie took a minute to compose a group text while we sat there in the car. I felt my breathing smooth out.

Thank you, God, for my family, and for the joy they bring into my life.

Seconds after she hit send, her phone began chiming. Aunt Kassie smiled big.

"Looks like we got us a Comedy Night tonight!"

Carroway Comedy Nights have been a tradition for our family

since back when our dads were kids. Whenever someone was stressed—either from work, school, or for some medical reason, our family would gather together and sing, dance, tell jokes, and basically be silly so that everyone would have a chance to laugh till they cry, fall on the floor, or pee their pants.

Mamaw Kat always quotes this Bible verse before the night begins:

A cheerful heart is good medicine, but a crushed spirit dries up the bones.

PROVERBS 17:22

As we began our comedy night that evening, I wondered if that was what had happened to me out on that school field. Was my spirit broken—or starting to break—when I realized that Mrs. Mellon wouldn't be able to help with the end-of-year project? I sure felt weak out there, lying in the rain. Was that why I couldn't breathe? Was Lola right about me having a panic attack?

"Thank y'all for coming on short notice," Aunt Kassie addressed the crowd of Carroways, who were all standing around in the kitchen. "Before we start the evening, we must congratulate Allie for being voted Student Project Manager of the Ouachita Middle School's year-end project today."

My family clapped, and some of the little kids—and my Papaw Ray—whooped and hollered.

"Allie, would you like to say some words?"

Oh, man. Usually words just pour out of me, but after the events of this day, I could only think of one.

"Help."

Then I sat down on a barstool. The family stared in my direction, and it wasn't until Kendall said the next thing that everyone understood.

"Mrs. Mellon had her baby today, so Miss Lewis is takin' over as faculty advisor."

My family knows the Lewis reputation, so there were gasps and head shakes galore.

Mom came up and began to rub my shoulders. "Allie, you didn't tell me about Miss Lewis. This is going to be a challenge, isn't it?"

I nodded. "That's why I said help."

Aunt Kassie waved a large mixing spoon in the air. "That's why we called an emergency comedy night."

"A cheerful heart is good medicine," Mamaw said. "And mac and cheese helps too." She pulled aluminum foil off a casserole dish and uncovered my favorite food in the entire world.

"We'll help you cheer up," my little cousin Chase said. "I can do a drum solo for you."

"And I invented a new game that we're gonna play tonight!" My Great Uncle Saul is a genius at creating weird games. The way he does it is simple; he just turns anything into a competition—like flinging fish guts into a bucket, playing hide and seek in model homes, slurping out words in alphabet soup, and today's game—spitting plastic Easter eggs into a kiddie basketball hoop.

"It's just like playing horse," Uncle Saul said. "Only you have an Easter egg, see, and you put it in your mouth, and then you skip, jump, or whatever, and you spit the egg through the hoop. If you make it, the next person has to do *exactly* what you did, and if they fail, they get an h. First person to spell 'horse' loses."

Uncle Saul just stood there with this huge grin on his face, and everyone else looked horrified.

"Sounds a little unsanitary," Mom said.

Uncle Saul brushed away her comment. "No way, Maggie Mae. We all got different egg colors, so we don't share spit."

Still, it sounded gross to me. But Uncle Saul's games never fail to make us laugh, so why not?

"Okay, but how about we play 'pig' so it's shorter?" Aunt Kassie grimaced.

"And less spit," Mom said.

"Pig it is!" Uncle Saul said. "Who's in?"

It was mostly just the kids and the dads who played. We had to breathe deep and then blow out hard for the eggs to go anywhere. I got to P-I fast, and I wasn't sure if I could finish because I was laughing so hard. Uncle Josiah (Lola and Ruby's dad) leaped around the room like a frog, then turned a somersault before blowing his egg successfully through the hoop from five feet away. Hazel Mae, Ellie, and T-Rex added to the humor by barking and chasing the eggs after they left our mouths. T-Rex picked one up with his mouth and brought it over to Hunter.

"Thanks, boy." Hunter took the green egg out of T-Rex's mouth and put it in his.

"Hunter!" Aunt Kassie yelled. "That is gross!"

"It's okay. I didn't brush my teeth today."

And with that, Hunter leaped around, even managed to croak a couple of times, leaned back, and "poofed" his egg through the hoop!

Everyone collapsed on the floor laughing—that kind of laugh that makes your stomach hurt.

"Now, didn't I tell ya that game was a winner?" Uncle Saul began to gather the spit eggs into a big trash bag.

"I'll save these at my house for the next time," he said.

"Give them to *me*." Aunt Kassie rushed Uncle Saul and pulled the bag away from him. "I'll be disinfecting these in the dishwasher first."

"And somebody needs to mop the spit marks off the floor," Mom said.

"Aww, they've practically evaporated," said Uncle Saul as he wiped a couple of spots with an old handkerchief he pulled from his pocket.

"I don't know if I can even eat now," Hunter said. "My stomach's like a brick."

"I can't eat anything *except* mac and cheese," I rubbed my jaw. "I think my cheeks hurt worse than my stomach."

"Okay, then, let's say grace and get this dinner started." My dad, who had opted out of the Easter egg spitting game so he could grill the burgers, took off his ball cap and bowed his head. We all bowed too.

"Father, thank you for the gift of laughter, and for this crazy, but wonderful family. Thank you for the food and for all the blessings you provide, and we pray that you will help our Allie-girl as she takes on a big project for her school. We know you will be with her every step of the way, guiding, teaching, and encouraging her. In Jesus' name, amen."

I looked up at Dad and smiled. "Thanks, Dad. I need all the help I can get."

"Hey! I have an idea," Uncle Saul said. "We can have an Easter Egg Spitting Basketball Booth at the carnival!"

"NO!" we all yelled.

"Just tryin' to help," Uncle Saul said, with a big grin.

Our family is big, so a lot of the time when we aren't in front of the cameras, we have our meals buffet style. And while I was lined up, waiting for my turn to fill my plate with food, I had lots of offers of help for the carnival.

"You know you can count on your family for anything,"

Mamaw Kat said. "Ruby already talked to me about her and I headin' up a bake sale."

"And I love to groom animals," Aunt Janie added. "We can have a 'Dog Spa' booth, where they can get a makeover!"

"I love that idea," Lola said. "I can make some more camo bandannas to sell, and we can put the Carroway logo on them."

Ideas just kept flowing, and I was encouraged. I had no doubt the Carroway family could pull off this carnival and dog show all by themselves.

The only problem was, we weren't going to be by ourselves. We had a whole student body to include in the planning, and then there was Miss Lewis—who would probably hate *all* these ideas.

I mean—she would probably *dislike* them.

Strongly.

After dinner, it was time for skits. There were the classic Carroway skits that show up at every comedy night—like the ones starring the "allibeaver"—a monster that's half alligator and half beaver—that supposedly lives in the lake at our local summer camp. Tonight's allibeaver skit featured Hunter, with duct tape, wrapping the allibeaver (my dad) in a chair, and then feeding him a S'more while telling him a story of the "Doomsberry Giant"—a red-haired, Goliath-type beast—that feeds on allibeavers.

I loved that one.

"Sometimes it's fun to act out your fears," Mamaw Kat said, and she winked my way.

"Okay then, I'd like to perform a skit." I stood and walked up to the front of the room. "But first, I need to talk to Kendall."

I ran over to Kendall and whispered in her ear. "I have an idea for a monster."

"While we're waitin', anyone want pie?" Mamaw moved toward the desserts that filled up the counter of the kitchen island.

"ME!" Hunter popped up.

"You better watch out, son. You eat too much pie and your arms could grow another two inches tonight." Uncle Wayne followed Hunter into the kitchen.

"What's your idea?" Kendall asked.

"Let's call it the . . . Lewis-Beetle. And when teachers get bitten by it, they turn grouchy and give everyone detention. And the only way they can be cured is if someone puts a pie in their face."

"I love it! Do we have whipped cream in the kitchen?"

I scrunched my eyebrows together. "Is this not a Carroway house? Of course, we have whipped cream."

Kendall and I planned the logistics of the skit while everyone stuffed themselves full of dessert.

"Okay, people, I'm ready to perform my skit, and I think it will help me deal with my greatest fear."

Everyone rushed to take their seats.

"Ooh, maybe this will be a new classic," Dad said.

I straightened up, and clasped my hands in front of me.

"I'd like to tell you a story about a pest that is taking over Louisiana."

I opened my eyes wide and scrunched up my nose and lips.

"It hovers near school grounds, and there is no bug-repellent that will keep it away."

I held my index finger up.

"This pest is called . . . the Lewis-Beetle, and its bite is worse than deadly, because, if you get bitten by this beetle— you will *never* die. Instead, you will become a grouchy teacher and you will scare students . . . *forever!*"

I filled the room with a devilish laugh.

My little cousin Chase shrieked, "Like a zombie teacher?!?"

"Yes," I said, and I leaned forward toward the crowd. "You will become a zombie teacher."

Mamaw Kat put both her hands on her cheeks and gasped, "The horrors!"

My parents and aunts and uncles chuckled, but only a little.

"I think *all* my teachers were zombies," Uncle Saul said.

"Well, the Lewis-Beetle has been around a *long* time," I said. "And *all* of us have been impacted in some way. But—good news. Today, scientists announced that they have discovered a cure for the Lewis-Beetle bite, one that will reverse the curse and make the grouchy teacher nice again."

"What is it?" Chase asked. He was curled up in a tight little ball in Uncle Saul's lap.

"Well, I'm going to tell you right now."

I nodded at Kendall to give her the cue, and then I took my hand and slapped my left forearm.

"Ouch! What *was* that?" I pulled my hand away, and inspected the imaginary bite. "OH, NO!!!! Something bit me!" I put my face closer to my arm. "And the bite is the shape of, oh, no, a jaggedy letter Z!"

Chase screamed, "ZOMBIE!"

"Allie," Mom said. "Tone it down a little. This is *comedy* night, you know."

"Trust me, Mom, it's about to turn hilarious."

I paced back and forth in front of the room. "What am I

going to do? I think I've been bit by the Lewis-Beetle!" I slapped a hand over my heart. "Wait, I know what I have to do." I put on my best grumpy face and pointed at my dad. "I have to give YOU detention!" Then I pointed to Papaw Ray. "And you, sir, DETENTION!" Then I pointed to Aunt Janie. "And you, young lady, you need to STOP saying UMMMMMM!" Then I walked toward Uncle Wayne. "Drop down and give me 20 pushups! NOW!"

And, on that cue, Kendall came out of the kitchen, carrying the cure. She shot by me, like a flash, and shoved a whipped cream pie in my face.

The Carroway family erupted in laughter as the pie tin fell to the floor and left my cream-covered face staring at them. I took my fingers and pulled whipped cream from my eye sockets. Then I stuck out my tongue, licked my lips, and smiled. A pie in the face gets laughs no matter what.

"Students," I said, "I feel all tingly!" I looked down at my arm. "And my bite is gone!"

"Thank you, Jesus!" Chase yelled.

"And I feel . . . different. In fact, I feel joyful, and happy, and . . . nice. Okay, students! No more detention! No more pushups, and you can say UMMMM as much as you like."

Everyone cheered.

I wiped some cream off my cheeks and licked it off my fingers.

"And now, anytime you see a teacher who looks like they've been bitten by the Lewis-Beetle, you know what to do to cure them. The End."

"Allie, what am I going to do with you?" Mom came over with a paper towel and wiped some whipped cream off the floor.

I shrugged. "What? It's a fictional story. Any similarity to real persons, living or dead, is purely coincidental."

She shook her head. "I know Miss Lewis can be difficult at times, but really . . . a Lewis-Beetle?"

"At *times*?" Dad replied. "Do you remember Cody's detention year?"

"I'm sorry, Mom," I said. "Mamaw said it helps to act out your fears, and I do feel a little less scared now."

"Sounds like you and this Miss Lewis could use some prayer," Papaw Ray said.

"Yeah. We need lots. It's a big project, and I am worried that we won't get along."

"Well," Papaw Ray said. "Go clean up your face and then we'll have a family prayer."

"Yes, sir."

I made my way to the bathroom, and my girl cousins followed me.

"That was hilarious," Kendall licked some whipped cream off her fingers. "I never knew how satisfying it would be to hit you in the face with a pie."

Ruby handed me a washcloth. "The funniest part was when the tin fell and we saw all the features of your face, but they were all creamy."

"I almost peed my pants right then," Lola said.

I wiped the excess cream from my face and then splashed more water to finally get everything off.

"I wish I could have seen that. It just looked goopy from my end."

"Well, I'm about to give you your wish." Lola pulled her phone out so I could see it. "I videoed the whole thing."

CHAPTER 13

0600

Comedy night ended early, because it was a school night. I was thankful for Papaw Ray and his prayer for me, that I would have strength and courage to follow through on my commitment as Student Project Manager—even though God had thrown me a curveball.

"Wait—" I called out quickly, after we all said amen. "God threw me the curveball? Isn't the devil the one who does that?"

"Depends," Papaw had said. "God knows what we need more than we do, and maybe he knows that right now you need a little stretchin.' Smooth isn't always promised to us, Allie-girl. Just ask the prophets, the disciples, and Jesus—for that matter. They sure didn't have it smooth sailin.'"

The next morning, while Mom was driving me to school for my 0600 meeting, I rolled my eyes, remembering Papaw's words.

Stretchin'.

That didn't sound fun at all.

Mom—who was in her sweats and oversized T-shirt—put the SUV in park and rested her head on her arms on the steering wheel. "I need coffee."

I don't drink coffee, but I could feel her pain. "Thanks for bringing me, Mom. I know it was early. See what happens when the Lewis-Beetle bites? Everyone suffers."

Mom laughed and got out of the car. I flopped out on the other side, and she came around and gave me a warm hug before she sent me off to Room 220.

"Don't hit her with a pie, okay? Prayer is the real cure."

"Okay," I said. "I'll try not to."

"Allie . . ."

I smiled. "Just kidding." And then I ran off toward the meeting, expecting torture of some kind.

Okay, Lord, bring on the stretchin'.

I pulled the door open. It seemed heavier than usual.

"Come on in, Carroway. It's six o'clock straight up, so we'll have to work on your punctuality, but at least you're here."

Miss Lewis stood by her desk, dressed for work already, in navy blue slacks and a red blouse. Her brown, shoulder-length hair was perfectly styled in layers, with some flippy ends curling out here and there. She was even wearing makeup. Apparently, *she* wasn't going to be doing pushups.

"Let's see . . ." Miss Lewis reached into a familiar-looking white bag. "Are you a glaze, cake, or apple fritter kind of girl?"

Donuts?

She walked over and handed me the bag. "I got an assortment. I know you have nut allergies, so I opted for sprinkles on the cake. Oh, and I have another bag of donut holes if you like those."

"Thank you." I opened and stared into the bag. I love *every* kind of donut. And I especially like donut holes.

I reached in and pulled out a glazed twist. "I'll start with this one." I took a bite. Pure goodness.

The door behind me squeaked open. I turned, and almost choked on the glaze when I came eye to eye with Madison Doonsberry.

Madison grinned much too big to be appropriate. "Good morning, Allie."

I swallowed the brick in my throat. "Good morning."

"You're two minutes late, Doonsberry," Miss Lewis said. "We'll have to work on that. But at least you beat your principal."

As if on cue, Mr. Langley came breezing through the door, checking his watch.

He put his hand out. "Megan, I know, fifteen minutes early is "on time" for you, but it couldn't be helped. I was dealing with a broken sprinkler that was threatening to flood the parking lot."

Miss Lewis sighed. "That's fine, Daniel. These ladies just arrived, and we can't get in until 6:30 anyway."

"Get in?" I asked. "Are we going somewhere?"

Miss Lewis walked over to a worktable at the side of the room that had several chairs pulled up to it. She sat down in one of the chairs. "You all can have a seat." She gestured to the extra chairs. It was amusing watching Mr. Langley try to fold his long legs under the table.

"We're going to visit my best friend—Mrs. Mellon—in the hospital, just as soon as she's done with breakfast."

Best friend?!?

"How is Mrs. Mellon doing?" Madison asked. A nice question, which surprised me.

"She's tired, but she's a typical teacher. She can't focus on resting until she gets her lesson plans in for the sub. So, we're going to pick those up, and she arranged to get us in early, so she can hand off all the information we need to get this project underway."

"Oh," was all I could say. I took another bite of my donut. So many shockers, and it wasn't even 6:15 yet!

"Do you have permission to take these students off campus?" Mr. Langley tried to maneuver his legs under the table and ended up pushing it toward Miss Lewis instead.

Miss Lewis got up, walked to her desk, and pulled a phone out of her purse. "They both have off-campus waivers signed for fieldtrips, and just to be safe, I texted both parents last night and have approval right here." She tapped her phone.

"You texted my mom last night?" The twisted glaze was now twisting in my esophagus. Did Miss Lewis text my mom during comedy night, and possibly even during the Lewis-Beetle skit?

Miss Lewis nodded. "Yes, did she not tell you?"

"No. But we were having a big family get-together, so I was hanging out with my cousins. She probably just forgot."

Madison piped up at that. "I just love your cousins. I hear you all laughing when I walk by that Lickety Split clubhouse of yours." Then she flipped her hair, crossed her arms in front of herself, and looked down at the ground.

Madison was dressed like Lola would be if she had somewhere to be at 0600. Red dress dotted with tan mini-flowers, a tan cardigan sweater, and ankle high boots that matched the sweater and flowers.

"Do you two live in the same neighborhood?" Miss Lewis gathered some spiral notebooks from her desk and plunked them down in front of both Madison and me.

"I actually live in Allie's old house, though it hardly looks the same inside." Madison smirked.

Miss Lewis raised an eyebrow at Madison. "I see. Well, perhaps living near each other will come in handy over the next two months."

I doubt it. It's been a nightmare so far.

I cleared my throat. "I don't think I understand."

Miss Lewis sat down and put both elbows on the table. She rested her chin on her clasped hands. "Allie, I was very impressed with your idea for the carnival and dog show. So impressed, that I was going to offer to help Mrs. Mellon with

77

it this year, because I could tell this was going to be a bigger undertaking than normal. Well, then she had to go and give birth. But it's still a big project. And then Madison arrived at our school yesterday, with some big ideas, and a celebrity dad who can pull in some resources."

I began to sweat as Miss Lewis continued.

"And then I seriously considered your note from yesterday . . ."

Ugh. That wasn't my note!

". . . and I thought it would be a great idea to add Madison to the steering committee, since she didn't get a chance to run in the election."

Mr. Langley bit into a powdered donut, sending a covering of white all over his blue dress shirt.

"And isn't it just icing on the cake that you already know each other and live in the same neighborhood?"

Madison scooched in her chair, eyes beaming. "Oh, Miss Lewis, I am so honored that you would invite me to serve the school in this capacity."

"Well, the final decision is up to Allie." Miss Lewis searched my eyes, and I hoped she wasn't using some super-power where she could read minds or emotions. Because if she was, she would be seeing a girl throwing an internal temper tantrum.

"What do you say, Allie?"

Miss Lewis leaned in toward me

Normally, I tell it like it is. And if this were a "normal" situation, I would have said, "NO WAY!"

But Miss Lewis was staring me down, so all that came out was, "I think that is a great idea."

CHAPTER 14

Baby Mellon

The car ride to the hospital was a nightmare. I was seated next to Madison in the back of Miss Lewis's red Volkswagen Beetle. Not much space to breathe. I wondered how Mr. Langley was managing to cram his legs in the front, but at least he didn't have to be squished next to someone who hated him.

I kinda got a laugh out of the fact that Miss Lewis drove a beetle, though.

"We're here to see Christie Mellon in the OB ward," Miss Lewis said to the clerk at the hospital information window. "We have prior permission."

The clerk looked us over, and checked Mr. Langley's and Miss Lewis's ID. "When you get in there, you can only have two in at a time."

"Oh? That's unfortunate. We have an important planning meeting." Miss Lewis gave that stern, military face to the clerk.

She immediately backed off. "Fine, then. But only one adult at a time."

The clerk buzzed the door open.

"I'll sit in the waiting area and keep Greg company if he's here." Mr. Langley took off to the left where the signs pointed to the lobby.

Miss Lewis, Madison, and I made our way through the echo-y hallways and finally reached the elevator that took us to the OB ward on the 4th floor. The first thing we saw when we stepped out was the baby nursery.

"Aww, look how cute they are!" Madison rushed to the window and made little googly noises at the babies.

"Mrs. Mellon's baby won't be in there," Miss Lewis said. "The NICU is around the corner."" Miss Lewis and I walked over to the window to join Madison.

"See that one?" Miss Lewis pointed to a baby wrapped in a blue blanket wearing a matching beanie. "It says he's 9 pounds, 3 ounces. Subtract 7.9 pounds, and you have little Bethany."

"Wow." That's all I could say, and then I said a silent prayer. *Help her grow healthy, Lord. This must be so scary for her family.*

Miss Lewis checked her watch. "Okay, troops, let's move. We don't have much time."

We worked our way around a couple of corners, and came upon the nurses' station.

"Hello, again," a kind-looking, middle-aged nurse said to Miss Lewis. "Your friend is doing a little better today. She slept surprisingly well, considering that ordeal yesterday."

Miss Lewis grinned at the nurse.

"Thank you. We won't tire her out, I promise. In fact, she'll probably be energized seeing students."

We stepped lightly into room 245. The overhead light was off and a curtain was drawn across the middle of the room.

Miss Lewis stepped around to the other side.

"Are you up, Christie? I brought visitors."

It suddenly occurred to me that I should have brought flowers or a card or something. But, hey—I thought I'd be running laps or something when this day started.

I poked my head around the curtain, and to my surprise, Mrs. Mellon was sitting up, eating Jell-O, with a little bit of a smile on her face.

"Allie, it's so good to see you. I'm so sorry I let you down right from the get-go on this project."

Her face was pale, and she had dark circles under her eyes, but you could still see her zest for life.

"It's okay," I said. "The most important thing is that you and the baby are healthy."

Mrs. Mellon started crying a little, and she wiped an escaping tear off her cheek with her fingers. "I'm fine," she said. "But please, pray for Bethany. She's so little, and there are so many complications."

"I will. And I'll ask my whole family to pray too. Some of the kids and I prayed for you in the quad when they were wheeling you out."

Mrs. Mellon wiped another tear. "Bless you, sweet girl. I know that made a difference."

Madison stepped up from behind me.

"Hello, my name is Madison Doonsberry. I just started attending OMS yesterday. My brother, Parker, is in your class."

Mrs. Mellon sniffed and then grinned a little. "Nice to meet you, Madison. My husband loves your dad's show. He's an avid fisherman."

"Thank you," Madison said. "I'll be sure to tell him that he has another fan." The way she emphasized *another* was kind of annoying.

Miss Lewis grabbed a chair from the corner of the room and dragged it over close to Mrs. Mellon.

"Madison is going to help us on the project as part of the steering committee. I'm thinking it will take quite a few extra people to fill your shoes." She fluffed Mrs. Mellon's pillow, and leaned back in her chair. "You're looking very tired, friend. Are you sure this meeting isn't going to be too much for you?"

So they really are friends?

"It's fine," Mrs. Mellon said. "Actually, it's going to be easy. All I have to do is give you one thing" She turned to me. "Allie, can you reach my bag over there?" I retrieved the turquoise tote, and handed it over to Mrs. Mellon. She reached in, pulled out an overloaded key ring, and unhooked a little key.

"This will open the top drawer of the silver filing cabinet next to my desk. In that drawer you'll find multi-colored files, with all the information you need, including timelines, contacts, vendor lists, and past donors."

Miss Lewis took the key and weaved it onto her key ring. "Thanks, Megan. I'm so thankful you're organized."

"To a fault," Mrs. Mellon said. "I drive my husband crazy with all my color-coded files, drawers, and hangers, but hey—in this case it's going to pay off."

Mrs. Mellon adjusted her bed up a few notches, so she could sit straighter. "The only thing I don't know about is dog trainers. So I guess you're on your own there."

I nodded. "That's no problem. I'm good friends with Mr. Felix at the animal shelter, and I think he's a trainer."

"Well," Mrs. Mellon took one more bite of her Jell-O and then pushed her food tray to the side. "It looks like you have the start of a really strong team. I know Ronnie and Samara will be great too. I wish I could promise to be there on the day of the event, but I just don't know yet with all the care that Bethany needs. They're telling me she might be in the hospital for four months."

I gulped. "Four? Isn't that expensive?"

"It's *beyond* expensive. But I'm trying not to think too much about that yet. We just need to get Bethany through one day at a time. We almost lost her yesterday." The tears started again, and this time they didn't stop. Miss Lewis stood up and leaned over to hug Mrs. Mellon.

"We're going to let you rest, Christie. Don't worry about a thing. God is taking care of every big thing and every small thing."

"Thank you. And thank you all for coming." Mrs. Mellon kept sobbing, so I didn't say anything. I just patted her shoulder and moved out of the room. Madison followed. We waited in silence for a couple of minutes, and finally Miss Lewis emerged—her eyes red from crying.

She straightened her blouse and wiped a tear that had made its way to her chin.

"So, would you girls like to see some small things that God is taking care of?"

She didn't wait for our answer, but instead took off down the hallway. Madison and I had to jog to keep up.

We finally landed at some double doors. Miss Lewis picked up a phone receiver from the wall and waited for someone to answer.

"Yes, this is Megan Lewis. We're here to see Baby Mellon."

Hearing her say Baby Mellon made me laugh to myself. When we first found out that Mrs. Mellon was pregnant, Hunter had joked that they should name the child "Water." My cousins and I groaned.

"But you know that'll be the kid's nickname, so why not?"

I'm glad Mrs. Mellon and her husband have better name taste than Hunter.

The double doors opened, and we entered the NICU hallway. There was a large window on the left side. I took a couple slow steps, but was reluctant to peek in.

"It's okay," Miss Lewis said. "We have special permission to be here, but only for a few minutes."

I didn't understand why they were allowing a couple of middle school girls into such a sacred place in the hospital. But I stepped forward and put my face near the glass.

A nurse stood next to a large clear case with holes in it. She smiled and gestured toward the tiniest baby I'd ever seen—it seemed like she was not much bigger than a mouse! A mask was strapped to her little mouth, and a tube was attached to that. It looked like IV fluids were entering her body through her umbilical cord area, and wired stickers were placed all over her chest, feet, arms, wrists, and legs.

"She's classified as a micro-preemie," Miss Lewis said. "She needs help with just about everything—breathing, eating, keeping cool and warm . . ."

So helpless.

Madison put her hand up on the window. "Welcome to the world, Mini-Mellon. I hope you like it here."

"She will." Miss Mellon rested her forehead on the glass. "She's had a rough start, but things will improve every day."

Madison took her hand down and sighed. "But there are no guarantees." She turned, walked to the other side of the hallway, leaned against the wall, and slid her back down to the ground. She pulled a phone out of her tote bag and stared at the screen, like she was expecting a text or a call or something.

I figured I'd give her some privacy, so I turned back to Baby Mellon.

Be still and know that I am God.

That Bible verse—one of my favorites—popped into my brain, and it described this little one so accurately. It seemed so easy for her to be still—after all, she couldn't walk or talk or do anything productive at all. Was she having a conversation with God as I watched her at this moment? Did she know she was safe in the hands of Jesus?

I hope so, God. Please help her know that you are her refuge and strength. Don't let her feel afraid.

The nurse pointed to the clock on the wall. Miss Lewis nodded. "Okay, girls, time's up. Let's go find Mr. Langley and get back to school."

Mr. Langley and Mrs. Mellon's husband, Greg, were sitting on a cushioned bench, eating muffins and drinking coffee. Mr. Mellon's hair was sticking up all over, and it wasn't in a stylish, bedhead sort of way either.

"Thanks for coming. I know Christie loved seeing all of you. She wanted so much to finish out the school year, and I know she would have wanted to work with you, Allie, on the school project."

"Thanks, Mr. Mellon." I wanted to add that I *really* wanted to work with her too and how disappointed I was, but Miss Lewis was standing right there.

"I'll be back tonight, Greg." Miss Lewis tapped on her phone screen. "Text me a list of things she needs and I'll bring them."

Mr. Mellon stood and ran his hand through his hair mess. "Thanks, Megan. She didn't exactly get a chance to pack for her trip here, so I'm sure she'll need something."

"I'm here to help with whatever you need." She reached over and put her hand on Mr. Mellon's shoulder. "Everything's going to be okay."

"Same goes for me, Greg," Mr. Langley said. "Let me know what you need. You have an OMS family who wants to help too."

"I appreciate that."

Miss Lewis looked down at her watch. "Bell rings in twenty minutes."

And with that, we all ran-walked to the Lewis Beetle.

CHAPTER 15

Steering into a Brick Wall

Once we were at school, it was like I had a sign on my forehead that said "Suggestion Box." Students who had never spoken to me before came up to me all morning to put in their two cents about the carnival and dog show.

"Can we have a special category just for Chiweenies?" Rachel Long asked. "I have four, and they are sooo cute. They're just not the smartest, so it may not be fair to put them up against other dogs."

"I don't know, but I will consider it." I tried to think if I'd ever seen a Chiweenie before. Was that a cross between a Chihuahua and a dachshund? Weird.

Jimmy Caruthers pulled me aside during our nutrition break. "We simply must make the Catahoula a mascot at the ceremonies. It *is* the Louisiana state dog, after all."

"Jimmy, do you know anyone who owns a Cata . . . What did you call it?"

"Catahoula. Like the Parish name. And no, I don't know anyone who has one."

"Oh. Okay. I'll consider it."

Dog show suggestions flew at me all the way until lunchtime. And a little fear began to rise in my belly. I thought I knew a lot about dogs, but clearly, I was wrong.

I took out my spiral notebook and scrawled a few notes:

- Google "Catahoula."
- Call Mr. Felix. Ask him about dogs.

That will be one long phone interview!

By lunch, and time for the first steering committee meeting, I had filled five pages with questions, suggestions, and . . . prayers, like this:

Oh, no, God, what have I gotten myself into?

The library was the location for the steering committee meeting, but I stopped by the cousin lunch table before I ran over.

"We're excited for you, Allie!" Ruby smiled big and handed me a large cookie, wrapped in plastic wrap. "You can share bites with the committee, and if they like it, tell them I can make a few hundred for the carnival."

"I can't wait to take T-Rex to the special dog training!" Hunter reached over to pick up his water bottle, but knocked it over onto the ground. "Aaaack! I did it again!"

"Here, Hunter, you can have mine." Kendall rolled her eyes and slid her bottle over in front of Hunter.

"Sorry I can't have lunch with you guys, but if you want details about how the meeting went, I'll be in the Lickety Split at four o'clock, doing some homework. Come and hang out."

"We'll be there," Kendall said.

I turned to walk toward the library, and Lola caught up to me.

"Hey, Allie, I talked to Madison this morning at break, and she told me that she's on the steering committee. Is that true?"

Ugh. I did not want to get into that whole story right before the meeting. I stopped and tried not to make eye contact with Lola.

"Um, yeah. Miss Lewis thought it would be the right thing to do, so she asked me if it was okay, and I said yes."

Lola's eyes got big. "You did? Is it *really* okay with you? I mean, wow, first Miss Lewis, and now Madison?"

I fidgeted. Looked up at the sky, then down at the ground. Played with the plastic wrap on the cookie.

"Allie . . . I know you're struggling . . ."

"Okay, fine. I'll tell you. I'm freaking out. I'm in over my head and now I feel like I have a person swimming next to me who wants to watch me drown."

Lola put a hand on my shoulder. "You won't drown. You'll see. This is going to be the most memorable year-end project ever."

"Lola, tornadoes that destroy whole towns are 'memorable'."

I swung the library door open, and spotted the main "steerers" of the steering committee sitting at a round table in the center of the room. Samara James, Ronnie Alexander, Miss Lewis, and a scowling Madison all sat with their spiral notebooks open— pencils sharpened and ready to write.

"Glad you could make it, Carroway," Miss Lewis said. She had lost that gentle demeanor that she had at 0600 and now resembled the drill sergeant we all know and fear.

My heart skipped a beat, and I checked the clock on the wall. "I'm sorry, am I late?"

Miss Lewis shook her head. "No. You're straight up."

"What does that mean?"

"It means you're right on time," Madison said. "But that leaves no margin for error. We all hurried over and were here fifteen minutes ago."

"It's fine, Carroway. You can sit here." Miss Lewis tapped the back of an empty chair right next to her.

Well, at least it's not next to Madison.

True, it wasn't right next to her. But when I sat down, she was staring right at me from across the table.

Miss Lewis began the meeting.

"First, I want to congratulate Miss Carroway for her marvelous idea for raising funds for the animal shelter. The kids obviously loved the idea, and they have great confidence in you as a leader to vote you in as Student Project Manager." Then she turned to Ronnie and Samara. "You two had stellar ideas, also, that I'm sure will be used in future year-end events."

Miss Lewis then turned her attention to Madison. "Allie has invited Madison to join our team, and you'll soon see that it was a wise choice. We'll be adding more students after today, when we decide what subcommittees we need to pull this thing off."

I invited her? Well, that's a stretch.

Madison piped up, "I'd like to volunteer to handle fundraising."

"Fundraising?" Samara James' eyebrows shot up. "That's the last thing people usually volunteer for."

Madison tilted her head to the side. "But that's the most important thing—don't you think? I mean, that's why we're doing this in the first place, right? To raise funds?"

"Sure," Samara said.

"Well, then, I think since I have a dad who's on television, I should be in charge of that. I think donors will listen to me."

"Allie's on TV too," Ronnie added.

"Yeah," Madison said. "But the Carroways have been around this town forever. No offense—but people may be tired of them. My dad's show is the new exciting thing, so, why not take advantage of that?"

How dare she insult my family and make sense all at the same time!

"What if we have a drawing, and offer anyone who donates at least two-hundred dollars of goods or services to the carnival a chance to enter to be on *Lunker Law*?"

Miss Lewis cut in.

"Madison, that's a fabulous idea, but are you sure this is something your dad can offer?"

"Of course. He calls the shots on the show, and I know he's committed to helping the community—and his daughter." Madison put both hands on her heart.

I could tell that Samara and Ronnie thought it was a good idea too but didn't want to be the first to say anything. So I helped them out.

"That's good. I like it. Yes, Madison, you can be our fund-raising chairperson." I suddenly remembered the cookie. "You'll want to talk to my cousin Ruby about a bake sale. Take a bite of this, and I'm sure you'll agree it's the tastiest thing you've ever eaten."

I slid the cookie over to her, and she slid it back. "Oh, no, I could never think of poisoning my body with that much sugar. But I'll talk to her. I don't mind selling junk if it raises more money."

"I would love to head up decorations and promotion," Samara doodled away in her notebook. "And that includes painting a mural with our theme on it. What exactly is our theme again? I know it's a Canine Carnival and Dog Show, but do we want to use that as a subtitle and then come up with something catchier? I can design a logo if you like."

Logo. Huh. How about something with a big red tornado tearing up our school?

"I got it!" Ronnie poked his index finger up in the air. "How about OMS Bark Fest?"

We were all silent. I was stunned.

Ronnie continued, "You know, OMS, because it's at Ouachita Middle School. "Bark' because it's a dog thing, and "Fest" is short for festival . . ."

"We get it, Ronnie," Madison tapped her pencil and gave him a blank, bored stare.

"It's brilliant." Miss Lewis sort of mumbled and kept taking notes.

"I love it!" Samara dug in her backpack and pulled out some colored markers and started sketching on a new page. "And I have ideas for a logo already."

Madison turned her stare toward me. "What do *you* think, Allie. You're the SPM, so it's your call."

Yeah, sure. Leave the decision up to me, so if no one else in the school likes it, I take the heat.

"It sounds great," I said. "Bark Fest it is. And Samara, I'm sure my cousin Lola would love to help you with the mural."

"And I'd like to be the volunteer coordinator," Ronnie wrote the word "Volunteers" in big, bold letters on the front of his notebook. "I love making lists and recruiting people. You tell me what activities we're running, and I'll get you the people."

Miss Lewis lifted an accordion-style paper file box from the floor and opened it. She pulled out a stack of colorful folders and began parceling them out to each of us, based on what the label said.

"Here are some materials that will make your jobs easier. Madison, there are huge lists of names in there of people who have donated in the past. Ronnie, here are lists of the last few years' adult volunteers. And Samara—here are lists of supplies we already have stored in sheds and closets around the campus. Oh, and in that file is the name of a printing house in town that will do brochures, posters, and even T-shirts for a reasonable price."

"You okay, Carroway?" Miss Lewis raised an eyebrow in my direction. "I think we're off to a great start. Now, we just need to come up with a date for the event—I believe it's usually on a Saturday around the fourth weekend in May, right?"

"That would be May twenty-seventh." Madison scrolled the calendar on her phone. Then she looked up. "Eight weeks from this Saturday. We can really tear it up in that amount of time, right, Allie?"

"Tear it up?"

"It's an expression. It means we can do an awesome job."

"Of course," I said. "We *will* do an awesome job."

"Good." Miss Lewis smacked her hand on the table. "Let's schedule our next meeting for Monday. That will give you all a few days to recruit your team members and report back on your progress. Let's do it after school. Plan for three hours. I'll have some burgers delivered."

Madison, Ronnie, and Samara quickly packed up their stuff and returned to the quad for the remainder of the lunch hour. On my way out, Miss Lewis stopped me.

"Carroway, I made copies of these, and I also made electronic files." She handed me the rest of the colorful folders. "Go ahead and read through everything. I think we're going to need a few more subcommittees."

"Okay. Thanks." I took what must have been fifteen folders off her hands. It felt like I added a fifty-pound brick to my backpack.

"And for the record," Miss Lewis said. "I don't think people are tired of hearing about your family at all, so make sure you invite them to participate in the Bark Fest. Remember, one person's opinion about you does not reflect the whole of society."

I nodded. "Gotcha."

CHAPTER 16

Up a Tree

Those folders in my backpack weighed me down for the rest of the school day. Not physically though. Mentally.

You're doomed, Allie. What made you think you could be the one to head up this project? You have no experience at all, and you're already busy with homework and filming the show. This is going to be a flop. You may as well quit now.

It was like all those folders were pushing me into my desk, suffocating me, and finally, during math—our last subject of the day—Mr. Vicker, who was now our long-term sub, said something about it.

"Allie, do you feel alright? You don't seem like yourself."

Mr. Vicker had somehow managed to walk in front of my desk without me noticing.

"Oh, uh . . . I'm fine. Just daydreaming, I guess."

More like "day-worrying."

Mr. Vicker sighed. "I get it. It's been a rough week, and it's only Tuesday."

I grinned. "At least we have a nice long-term sub."

Mr. Vicker laughed. "Well, we'll see what you say in a few weeks. I've never had to make you do real work before. Now I have to prepare you for state testing, assign an English paper, *and* a science project, and—get this—the grades I give you will determine if you advance to the ninth grade or not. That should make you shiver in fear."

I kind of laughed too, but then my head and hands broke

94

out in tingles. "Really? You're gonna give me all that work, knowing that I have Bark Fest in eight weeks?"

"Bark Fest?"

"Yeah, that's what we're calling it. The OMS Bark Fest Carnival and Dog Show. All proceeds go to the West Monroe Animal Shelter."

"I love it. You kids are so creative."

"Can that count for the science project? I mean, the whole thing is an experiment." I grinned my most charming grin.

"No," Mr. Vicker said, "but nice try."

The bell finally rang to end the school day, and Aunt Janie—Lola's and Ruby's mom—came to pick us up.

"Your backpack is huge, Allie-gator. Throw it in the back."

I ran to the back of the SUV, pulled open the liftgate, and hoisted it in. And for some reason, I wanted to crawl in next to it, curl up in a ball, and not talk to anyone on the twenty-minute drive home.

That, I knew, would never fly with the cousins, so I didn't even try. I had barely buckled my seatbelt when they started in with the questions.

"So, tell us what happened," Kendall said. "Everyone was buzzin' at lunch about Madison Doonsberry's proclamation that someone's going to win a chance to be on her dad's show."

I just about lost my breath. "She's talking about that already?"

"It's all over social media," Lola said. "Check it out—here's her post on the FriendClips app."

Lola handed me her phone, and I read aloud the words on the screen:

Hello, Friends! I, Madison Doonsberry, have been tasked with raising funds for the West Monroe Animal Shelter at this year's OMS Bark Fest Carnival and Dog Show. Will you help me make this year's event the best ever? For every two-hundred dollars in goods or services you donate, you will be entered into a drawing, and the winner (to be announced at the carnival) will have a cameo appearance on the hottest reality show in Louisiana—*Lunker Law*! Follow the links below to donate, or call Ouachita Middle School for more details.

At the bottom of the post was a cute picture of a golden retriever puppy. How could anyone resist that?

"Click the link," Lola said. "She already has donations."

"Huh?" I clicked, and it took me to a funding page that showed a goal of . . . twenty thousand dollars? And two-thousand had already been raised? In three hours?

"Isn't social media amazing?" Kendall shook her head. "News spreads like wildfire."

"Wildfire *destroys* things," Aunt Janie said. "Why don't you pick a better simile?"

Kendall thought for a minute. "Stomach flu?"

"How about peanut butter?" Hunter rubbed his belly.

"Try again," I said. "Peanut butter will kill me."

"Sorry, Allie, but I'm hungry."

"So, the only things we can think of that spread quickly are bad?" Ruby fiddled with her orangey-red braid she had pulled over her right shoulder.

"Hmmm," Aunt Janie gave us a concerned look from the rearview. "I'd say that's something to consider when it comes to social media. I'd be careful with it if I were y'all."

I sat in the tan beanbag chair in the Lickety Split that after-noon and watched as donations increased on Madison's funding page.

She made it sound like she was the one in charge of the whole project!

I pulled up my FriendClips page—the one I had begged my mom to let me open just a couple of months ago, when I turned thirteen. The first week I posted a bunch of silly selfies and I "checked-in" everywhere I went. That got me an immediate lecture from my dad on the dangers of giving up my location to everyone on the Internet.

"But Dad, I only have twenty-five followers, and they're all family."

"I don't care," he said. "No more checkin' in."

So that kind of made me scared to post anything else.

I clicked back to Madison's personal FriendClips page. Four thousand fifty-five followers. *How can that be?*

I did a quick search for Parker Doonsberry—just to see if he was on.

No.

"Hey, Allie, Allie, Allie! Are you up there?"

It was Hunter. I put down my phone, pushed myself out of the beanbag chair, and stepped out onto the balcony.

"Hey, Hunter, come on up. You'll be happy to know I have food."

I had packed enough for an army, and told my mom and dad that I wouldn't be home for dinner since I had a ton of homework and project planning to do in the Split. Since we're living at my Aunt Kassie and Uncle Wayne's house till our new house is built, there are so many people at the dinner table, I would hardly be missed.

Hunter climbed up the spiral stairway, and when he got to the top, he greeted me by bonking me on the head with a cardboard tube.

"Wrapping Christmas presents in March?" I asked.

"This . . ." Hunter held the tube high in the air. ". . . is *not* a Christmas wrapping-paper weapon. It is a secret plan to make a fortune for the animal shelter." Hunter walked over to the writing desk, popped the plastic end off the cardboard tube, and pulled out some rolled-up papers. He spread them out, and put some books on the corners to keep the papers flat.

"This little baby is called the 'Dimple-Dunk 5000.'"

"A dunk tank?" I raised both palms toward the ceiling. "Hunter, we always do a dunk tank."

"Not one like this, we don't! This one is huge! It holds 5,000 gallons of water, the victim sits up higher, and the window is bigger so the people can see the person underwater better. It's also going to be painted in camo. I knew you'd appreciate that."

I checked out the plans. It looked like a dunk tank on steroids.

"I always feel a little sorry for the poor person who gets dunked over and over again. They look like a drowned rat."

"And in the Dimple-Dunk 5000, they'll look like a big-old drowned nutria rat!"

Hunter held his hands out to his sides. "It'll be amazing. And we can have people pay big for who they want to dunk the most. Think about how much we could make dunking Mr. Langley or Jared Strickland . . . or even Miss Lewis!"

"Yeah, Hunter, but the person would have to agree to be dunked for that to work."

"Use your leadership gift to talk them into it."

"Leadership gift?"

"Yeah. People don't win elections by a landslide if they don't have a leadership gift."

"Hey!" A voice called from below. "Is anyone up there? 'Cause I'm not climbin' if there isn't company."

Kendall.

I peeked my head over the railing. "Good timing, cousin! We're checking out Hunter's money-making idea for the Bark Fest."

Kendall came up, looked over the plans, and shook her head. "No way anyone is gettin' me in that thing."

I put one fist on my hip. "Oh, come on, Kendall. Think of your sweet little Ellie-dog. How would you feel if she was in a crowded, run-down shelter waiting on a family? Would you be willing to be dunked for her?"

Kendall rolled her eyes. "Okay, fine! You got me. I'll do it. But I won't like it!"

Hunter shot me a knowing glance. "See, I told you. Leadership gift. People naturally follow you."

"Tell that to Madison Doonsberry," I said. "She seems to think *she's* the leader of this project."

"Well, she's definitely aggressive." Kendall pulled out her phone. "Have you seen how many hits she's gotten on her FriendClips post? Like 4,000 or something like that."

"Helloooo! I have craft ideas!" Lola made her way up the stairs carrying what looked like several wooden boards. Ruby followed, lugging a tote filled with craft paint and little brushes.

Lola spread all her materials out on the 5-in-1 game table Mamaw had gotten for us at a garage sale.

"I miss our old Scripture boards that used to hang in the Diva," Lola began pulling little paint bottles out of the tote. "We need to see God's Word in big, colorful letters. So, I'm making new ones. Do y'all have any new favorite verses?" We all sat down on the cushy chairs to think.

"I don't know if we should use wooden boards again," I said. "Those last ones were mold traps."

Lola grinned. "I'm way ahead of you, Allie. These may look like wood, but they're plastic. See?" She held one up and flicked it with her fingernail, making a hollow sound. "I just painted them to look like wood."

"Pure craft genius," Kendall said. "You should make some of those and sell 'em at Bark Fest. You know, if you donate two-hundred dollars' worth of goods or services, your name will be put in the drawing . . ."

I put my hand out. "Hey, people, no Carroways on the competitor's show! Come on!"

"I was just kiddin'."

"Let's not change the subject." Lola scolded us with her paintbrush. "I want you to give me Bible verses." She took a pen and a pink post-it from the writing desk drawer and got ready to write.

"Psalm 46:10," I said. "Be still and know that I am God."

Lola jotted it down. "That's a good one for you, since I've never really known you to be still."

Ruby giggled. "God made her to be a back-flipping machine."

As she said that, I was wriggling in my chair. It *is* hard to be still.

"I saw Mrs. Mellon and her baby this morning," I said, "and all I could think of was how all that teeny-tiny baby can do is lay there and let people take care of her. She has no control over her life at all. And that verse popped into my head."

Lola nodded. "I feel out-of-control most of my life."

"I'm a control *freak*," Kendall said.

"And I feel like I'm losing control of this Bark Fest and it's only day one!" I punched my fist into the beanbag. "Lola, make that verse big and clear so I can look at it a lot over the next two months."

"You got it, Allie."

"Thanks." I pulled the many multicolored folders out of my backpack and held them up to show my cousins.

"Miss Lewis gave me these folders to read tonight. Do any of you know how to run a dog show?"

Ruby jumped to her feet. "I watch them on TV all the time! I can do that for you."

"Really? But what about your bake sale?"

Ruby grinned. "Mamaw can run that with one hand tied behind her back. Plus, I can still help her bake."

"Wow, thanks Ruby. I feel much better already."

Ruby took an empty folder from me, grabbed a pen, and labeled it 'Dog Show File."

"It'll be fun. Hey, you should schedule that dog clinic with a trainer soon, though, so the owners have plenty of time to work with their dogs. I know Max is a slow learner."

I pointed right at her. "Good call. I'm going to contact Mr. Felix right now and make a date."

I pulled up his contact information and dialed the number of the animal shelter.

"Hello, Allie!" Mr. Felix greeted me. "I was just telling the employees about your project and how it is going to help our dogs. Everyone is very excited!"

I smiled. "I'm happy to hear that! Everyone is excited on our end too. Hey, Mr. Felix, you're a dog trainer, right? Well, I was wondering if you would be willing to put on a clinic to teach kids how to train their dogs to do tricks and stuff . . . You would? That's the best! Can we pick a date a couple of weeks from now, like—say, Saturday, April 15th? . . . Kiroli Dog

Park? . . . That would be a perfect location. Okay, yes . . . that time works. My team and I will get the word out to the school and the rest of the community! Thank you, Mr. Felix. I'm looking forward to it!"

I hung up the phone, feeling confident again.

"April 15th, it is, at 9:00 am, Kiroli Dog Park. Can you all come?"

Kendall scrolled the calendar on her phone. "I've got no plans."

"Me either," Hunter said. "Except we'll miss our weekly Donuts-in-the-Split meeting."

"I'll bring donuts to the event," I said.

"Then it's a go for me and T-Rex."

"Hey, Lola," Kendall said. "When's Madison's birthday party? Isn't that on a Saturday?"

Lola looked up from her painting. "Oh, yeah. That's this Saturday, and I still feel a little funny about going."

"Did you get her a present yet?" Ruby asked.

Lola nodded. "I got her that same necklace I was wearing the other day since she liked it so much."

"And she shamelessly begged you for it." Kendall rolled her eyes.

"Well, that made the choice easy. I was also thinking of making her one of these Scripture boards, but I don't know what verse to put on it. Do any of you know if Madison is a Christian?"

"Parker told me that he accepted Jesus as his savior a year or so ago," I said. "I didn't ask about Madison."

"I don't get a Jesus vibe from her—that's for sure." Kendall got up, pulled a Bible from the bookshelf in the corner, and flipped through some pages.

"I've got a verse," Ruby chimed in. "How about 1 Peter 5:7: 'Give all your worries and cares to God, for he cares about you.'"

"I like it," Hunter said. "If she's a believer, it will be a good reminder. If she's not, it will give her something to think about."

"Okay, 1 Peter 5:7 it is." Lola agreed.

I sat down on the beanbag chair and sorted the stack of folders on the floor in front of me. My fingers began to tingle, and I yawned, to try to get a deep breath. It didn't come easy. I pulled my phone out and checked Madison's funding site again. Donations were up another thousand. It didn't seem like Madison Doonsberry had cares or worries at all. So far, everything she had done for this project was turning to gold.

"Hey, Lola . . ."

"Yeah, Allie?"

"Can you make an extra 1 Peter 5:7 for me? I think I need to hang it right . . . there." I pointed to the spot on the ceiling where I was staring.

CHAPTER 17

Party Pooper

I sat on my bed and flipped the calendar over to the new month. April 1st. My toes began to twitch as I realized the Bark Fest was getting closer. It was also April Fool's Day—and Madison Doonsberry's thirteenth birthday. How fitting, except that it was Parker's birthday too, and that didn't make sense at all.

I *wonder if Lola is nervous about going to the party.*

For some reason, I was nervous about Lola going to the party.

Hazel Mae poked her head though the bedroom doorway.

She ran in and jumped up on my lap. I cuddled her soft white furriness, and she licked me on the cheek. That gave me an idea.

Kendall was still asleep, *her* cheek in perfect licking position. If she didn't get up soon, she'd miss the Donuts-in-the-Split meeting. So I took Hazel Mae over there.

"Share some slobber with my cousin," I whispered. And Hazel Mae licked away.

Kendall's body immediately went into acrobat mode—her legs flipping around and arms waving.

"Ewww! Slime! What? Where? Wet! GROSS! UGH!" It was a hilarious sight.

"Allie—I'm glad you're amused. I thought I was drowning in a swamp!" She picked up her pillow and wiped her cheek with it. "How could you do that to me? I trust you to be a good roomie!"

I laughed. "I'm sorry. It's just you looked like you needed to wake up in a different way today. Hazel Mae loves you."

Kendall balled up her fists and wiped her eyes. "Well, I love her too, but I'm not a fan of her slobber." She swung her legs to the side of the bed and sat up. "Where's Ellie?"

"Don't know. Let's go find out and take the dogs for a walk. It's Donuts-in-the-Split day."

Just then a text came in from Lola:

> Family photo day at Kiroli Park. Sorry. Will
> miss Split meeting. Fill me in on info later.

Kiroli Park is a beautiful, wooded place in West Monroe that is home to a lake, walking trails, several playgrounds, and a dog park. Lola and Ruby's family go there every spring to take photos so they can have them printed and expertly framed for Aunt Janie in time for Mother's Day.

I texted Lola back.

> More donuts for us! Be careful at the party
> tonight. Take pics of Madison's room.

Lola returned with:

> I'll try.

"You wanna go for a walk?" I pulled out Hazel Mae's pink leash, and she bolted toward the closet.

"Hey—it's for your own good, since you can't stop terrorizing Madison's yard."

I hooked her up and waited as Kendall threw on some grubbies. "I hope we don't see anyone we know," she said.

"Well, we know *everyone* in this neighborhood, so that will only happen if we don't go out. But what kind of life is that?"

Kendall shook her head at me. "Let's go."

Just over the first little hill, we spied Parker Doonsberry.

Kendall pulled her sunglasses down from her head to her eyes. "Let's go back."

"Why? Don't you want to wish Parker a happy birthday?"

"Yes, but I want to improve my appearance before I do that."

I stopped and looked over at my cousin. "Kendall, do you really have a crush on Parker?"

Kendall licked her fingers, then ran them through her shoulder-length brown hair to smooth it down. "Oh, come on, Allie, doesn't every girl at school? He's so nice, and cute, and adorable, and well . . ."

Right at that moment, a "Hunter-train" zoomed in from behind, and chugged up the path to meet Parker.

"What is he *doing*?" I asked.

Kendall stopped and turned around. "He's creatin' a diversion, so I can go comb my hair and put on somethin' presentable. Gotta love that brother of mine."

I grabbed Kendall by the shoulder to stop her from walking away.

"No, he's not. They're coming right at us."

"Hey, girls! I gotta tell ya somethin'!" Hunter ran toward us, Parker following a bit behind.

Kendall breathed in a huge breath and then huffed and puffed it out. "Whatever."

We walked a few steps forward.

"What's goin' on Hunter?" Kendall asked.

Hunter stopped to catch his breath. "I forgot to tell you. Parker and I are hanging out together today. We're gonna race cars, play video games, and do other stuff that girls don't care about. So, I won't make it to our Split meeting. It's his thirteenth birthday today."

I smiled. "Yes, we know. Happy birthday, Parker."

Parker blushed a bit. "Thanks."

Kendall said nothing, which isn't like her at all.

"So, are you having a party like Madison?"

Parker put his hand out. "Oh, no, I don't like big parties. I prefer to just have fun with a friend or two."

"That must be so weird to always have your birthday on the same day as your sister."

Parker grinned. "It's okay. We like different things, so it always works out."

Parker turned his head. "Hi, Kendall. Have you written any songs lately?'

Kendall pulled her sunglasses back up on to her head. "How did you know I write songs?"

"Hunter told me. Did you know that I play the guitar?"

"You do?"

Kendall had let go of Ellie's leash and she didn't even notice when Ellie ran down toward the creek.

"Yeah. Maybe we could jam sometime. Like on that bench by the water." Parker pointed over in Ellie's direction. "I like playing music outside."

"Uh . . . sure," Kendall said.

"Hey, Parker, do you have a FriendClips account?" I pulled my phone out of my pocket. "I was just looking at Madison's the other day, and I tried to find you, but nothing came up on the search."

Parker shook his head. "Nah. I don't do social media. Plus, you have to be thirteen to open one of those accounts, and I just turned that today. Wait, did you say Madison has one?"

I turned my phone to show him.

"Great. Now I have to decide whether to tell my parents about that."

"Sorry," I said.

"Madison doesn't always follow the rules." Parker reached for my phone. "Do you mind if I read that last post?"

"Go right ahead."

Parker studied the screen, and then put a hand up to his forehead. "Oh, no, Madison, what were you *thinking*?"

"Is something the matter?"

Parker handed the phone back to me. "She just goes a little overboard sometimes with her enthusiasm. I'm pretty sure she hasn't checked with my dad to see if he can put the winner of a drawing on his show. He has a legal contract, and I know they're strict about content. He can't just make decisions like this without permission."

I stared down at the post, and clicked the link for the funding page. We were at four-thousand dollars.

"So, are you saying that she might not be able to follow through with her promise?"

Parker nodded. "That's right. But, don't worry. My dad's a great guy, and once he finds out about this, he'll do whatever he can to help. After he freaks out a minute."

"Do you think we can we be sued for falsely advertising a contest?" I asked.

Parker chuckled. "I have no idea, but my dad would— *Lunker Law*, you know?"

"Hahaha! That's a good one, Parker." Hunter laughed.

I couldn't join in on the joke. I just kept thinking about how we had already spent some of Madison's fundraising dollars on supplies for the Bark Fest.

And Kendall wasn't helping me one bit. She was just standing next to me in a daze.

"Well, we better be going," Parker said. "I'll think about how I'm going to mention this to my dad. If you could kind of keep it a secret, I'd really appreciate it."

I nodded. "Sure. Well, as secret as it can be with it out on social media. Just let me know what you decide, and we'll stop spending the funds till we figure things out."

"Sounds cool."

"See ya, girls!" Hunter waved, and then he and Parker turned and headed back toward the Doonsberry's house.

I picked up Hazel Mae and turned to the statue girl next to me. "Well, that was *very* interesting."

Kendall stared off in the distance. "I love him."

"What? You're nuts!" I reached out and gave Kendall a little push, which took her off balance.

"No, I really do."

"No, you don't. You don't even know him."

Kendall put one hand on her hip. "He's cute, kind, he has integrity, and he plays the guitar. What else is there to know?"

"Your dog has run away."

"WHAT?" Kendall came out of her trance, and she spun around in a circle. "Ellie! Where are you? Ellie!"

I shook my head. No one in the Carroway family could be allowed to fall in love with Parker Doonsberry. And no one— under any circumstances—could *ever* marry him—because that would make all of us Carroways relatives of Madison Doonsberry! And that was against the law. And that's not *Lunker Law*. It's Allie's Law!

Kendall and I found Ellie, and then, since Ruby, Lola, and Hunter were all gone, we skipped our meeting but went to the Lickety Split to work on plans for the Bark Fest. We chipped away at the task list for a couple of hours, but a few times I had to yell Kendall's name to pull her out of her Parker thoughts.

"I'm sorry, Allie, I just keep hearing this melody in my head, and I won't be able to concentrate until I can strum it out on my guitar."

She had reached her limit, so I cut her loose, with the promise that I would be the first one to hear her Parker love song.

After Kendall left, I found that I had lost *my* concentration too, so I burrowed into the soft, tan beanbag and stared at the ceiling.

Give all your worries and cares to God, for he cares about you.

Lola finished the Scripture board for me and had already hung it up! It was great timing, since after my chance meeting with Parker that morning I'd been feeling jittery and breathless. I'd already puffed on my inhaler as many times as I was allowed, but it didn't help. How were we going to fix this fundraising mess?

Lord, I'm really scared.

I was reminded of Lola's words. "This year-end project will be the most memorable one ever."

Yep. No Student Project Manager had ever been sued before. That would be memorable.

Be still and know that I am God.

I sat up, and crawled over to the wooden bookshelf in the corner of the Split. I pulled out a Bible and turned to Psalm 46.

God is our refuge and strength, always ready to help in times of trouble. So we will not fear when earthquakes come and the mountains crumble into the sea. Let the oceans roar and foam. Let the mountains tremble as the waters surge!

"Whoa, that's intense," I said out loud.

I skimmed down a bit, and another line jumped out at me.

The nations are in chaos, and their kingdoms crumble!

"Lord, this carnival is in chaos . . ."

God's voice thunders, and the earth melts. The Lord of Heaven's Armies is here among us. The God of Israel is our fortress . . . Be still and know that I am God.

"Who are you talking to?"
I jumped, and nearly threw the Bible across the room.
"Lola! You practically gave me a heart attack!"
Lola grabbed my arm and dragged me over to the beanbag. "I'm so sorry. I didn't know anyone was up here. What are you reading? What's so intense?"

"Chaos," I said. "Complete disorder and confusion. It's kind of where I am right now."

"Oh, dear, it must have been quite a morning for you. My morning was torture. You wouldn't believe the matching outfits Mom made us wear for the picture! At least it wasn't camo."

I nodded. "Yeah."

Lola got up and walked over to the craft table. "Anyway, I just came to get this. I had to let the paint dry." She picked up the Scripture board she had made for Madison. "I wish I could stay and help you, Allie, but I have to go get ready for the party." Lola sighed. "I've never gone to a party without one of my cousins. It feels weird."

"It'll be fine. I'm glad you're going. I need someone hanging out in the enemy's camp."

Lola's eyes opened wide. "What are you talking about?"

"Madison Doonsberry—birthday girl. I don't trust her, so it's good that you're close so you can keep an eye on her for me."

"That seems wrong, Allie. If I'm going to go to her party, it should be to honor her, not spy on her."

Gah. Lola was right. What did that Scripture say right out in front of our beloved Lickety Split?

Be devoted to one another in love. Honor one another above yourselves.

ROMANS 12:10

I hung my head. "I'm sorry. Forget about everything I just said, and just go have a fun time."

"Thanks. I'll see you tomorrow at church."

Lola gathered up her sign and clunked down the wood stairs. I sat back down on the beanbag and prayed for an attitude adjustment.

> Lord, I don't know why I'm so nervous about this
> project. It's just so big, and nothing's turning out like
> I hoped, and for some reason I have no confidence
> that it's gonna get better. I don't think I can do this
> on my own. Well, I know I can't do it on my own. I
> need your help, Lord. To know what's next. To know
> who to trust. So, Lord, when I stand up right now, I
> ask for strength! Please give me some confidence! I
> know you'll do it. In Jesus' name, amen.

For the next few hours, I mowed through those folders, reading every line. I got on the phone and booked vendors, ordered equipment, and I even mustered the courage to ask a carnival ride company if they would donate the use of a Ferris wheel for the day, and they said yes!

God was already at work, calming the chaos.

Or so I thought.

I checked the time on my phone—5:30 p.m.! And I was starving.

"Hazel Mae, let's go get some food . . . Hazel Mae?"

Hazel Mae had been sleeping soundly in the corner of the Split last time I checked.

What time *was* that when I checked?

Whenever it was, she was long gone now.

"Uh-oh. She better not be . . ."

I grabbed a plastic bag out of my backpack and sprinted toward the home of Madison Doonsberry.

As I approached my old house, I heard splashing, giggling, and other joyful party sounds. I poked my head around the side of the house, and there she was, being petted by a bunch of beautiful girls in swimsuits.

"Allie Carroway, is that you?" It was Madison's voice, and it was mocking me. I wanted to run, but she'd already seen me, so I put on my best smile and rounded the corner.

"Happy birthday, Madison. I'm sorry about my silly dog. I hope she didn't . . ."

"Oh, she *did*, but we cleaned it up, no problem. She's been a pure joy to have around. She even floated on the swim mat with Penny."

"Penny?"

"That's me," the girl with the shiny long brown hair sitting on the side of the pool said. "Your dog is so cute."

Lola held up her phone. "I tried texting you to let you know she was here, but you didn't answer."

"Oh, uh, I was on my phone a bunch, and I was really focused on carnival planning, so I guess I just missed it. I'll take Hazel Mae, and I'll let you get on with your party."

"You don't have to leave, Allie," Madison said. "I want you to meet my friends." She began gesturing to girls in all different places on the back patio. "That's Chloe over there, and Kaitlyn, Eve, Karly, and Veronica."

"Hello." I put up my hand to wave at everybody.

They waved back.

"We were just about to have cake. Would you like to join us? It's Reese's Peanut Butter Cup."

Huh. I thought you didn't like to eat junk.

Madison's hand flew to her forehead. "No, wait! You're allergic to nuts, right? Where are my manners? We could probably scrounge up a sugar cookie or something for you."

"Please stay, Allie," Karly said. "Madison was just telling us all about how she's helping you with the OMS carnival. It sounds like it's going to be great. You're so lucky to have Madison's star dad involved too."

Yeeeeaaah.

"I'm sorry," I said. "I have to go. I'm expected home for dinner. But thank you for the invite."

I pried Hazel Mae from Penny's grip.

"Happy birthday, Madison," I said, and then I ran as fast as I could back to the safety of Aunt Kassie and Uncle Wayne's house.

CHAPTER 18

No News = No News

I sent Lola lots of texts that night.

How's the party going?

Are they being nice to you?

Have you seen M.D.'s room yet?

Can you send me a picture?

Has anyone talked about me?

After text number thirty-two, I figured Lola's phone must have died, since out of all the cousins, she's the most text-y, and yet she hadn't replied even once.

"I'm gettin' nothin' from Lola," I said to Kendall as we brushed our teeth to get ready for bed. "You'd think she'd at least check her phone once or twice."

Kendall swished around some mouthwash and spit it out. "Waaah, that's minty!"

She sucked in a breath. "That would probably work just as good as an inhaler in a pinch."

I sniffed the mouthwash. "Hazel Mae needs to gargle with this. And, by the way, while you were writing love songs this afternoon, Hazel Mae and I crashed Madison's party."

"What?" Kendall grabbed me by the pajama sleeve and pulled me into our bedroom. She flung herself onto her bed, grabbed a pillow, and rested it on her crossed legs.

"Tell me all about it. Oh! Was Parker there?"

I threw my pillow at her. "Seriously? Is that all you can think about? I'm dealing with a bully who's trying to take over my project and all you can think of is Parker?"

Kendall twisted her face up. "Maybe. But you're my cousin, and I love you, so I'll try really hard to focus on that right now." She pressed her index and middle fingers from both hands into her temples, and closed her eyes. "Okay, tell me again what you're concerned about."

I sighed real hard. "Madison hates—I mean she dislikes me a whole bunch. Yet, she's working closely on this project with me. She's raising funds, promising a prize she can't deliver, and I feel like she's just waiting for me to mess up somewhere so she can ride in and take over."

Kendall kept her eyes closed for a minute and dug her elbows into her pillow.

"Kendall, am I boring you to sleep?"

She popped her eyes open. "No! I was just thinking about what you just told me."

I threw my hands up in the air.

"And?"

"And . . . I don't know. Maybe you *are* panicking a little. It probably just seems worse since you lost Mrs. Mellon as faculty advisor."

"It *is* worse."

Kendall laughed. "Oh, yeah." Then she got serious. "Hmmmm. I think you should talk to Mamaw."

My mood lightened. "That's a good idea. I wish we were out at her place right now."

One side of Kendall's mouth curved up. "Allie, she's downstairs watchin' chick flicks with our moms."

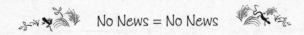
"What? Mamaw's here? I didn't know that! When did she get here?"

"When you were texting, about an hour ago. I guess you were more focused on that than I was on writin' my song, which—by the way—do you want to hear it?"

I jumped up off the bed. "Not now."

Kendall gave me a frowny-face.

"I'm sorry. I just have to talk to Mamaw."

I flew down the stairs, and in seconds I was wedged between my mom and Mamaw on the couch. They and my Aunt Kassie were munching on popcorn and watching an old musical.

I reached forward, grabbed the remote from the coffee table, and pressed pause.

"Allie! We were watchin' that!" Mom tried to wrestle the remote away from me.

"Yeah, but don't you need a snack break? I want to talk to Mamaw for a minute."

"I need Milk Duds," Aunt Kassie said, and she got up and headed for the kitchen.

Mom put up a finger. "Ten minutes. You know how I love my musicals." Then she headed toward Kassie and the Milk Duds.

Mamaw grabbed a blanket from the back of the couch and spread it over both of us.

"What's goin' on, Allie-girl? You still worried about the carnival?"

I pulled the blanket up to my neck. "Yeah. I think I'm getting stretched, like Papaw warned me about."

"That's uncomfortable. I'm sorry, darlin'."

I rested my head on her shoulder. "I'm mostly worried about Madison Doonsberry."

"Well, you should be. She's jealous of you, and that causes people to be real nasty."

I sat up straight. "Jealous? I don't think so."

"Well, I do. That girl's been through some pain, and the only one who can heal her is our Heavenly Father. But until she lets him in, she's got a God-shaped hole in her heart. So, like I said, pray for her, but stay alert."

"That isn't really soothing my spirit, Mamaw."

Mamaw put her arm around me and hugged me tight. "I'm sorry, sweet girl. But your family will always be here. No matter what happens, we'll always protect and support you. Got that?"

Warmth creeped from my toes all the way up to my cheeks. "Thanks, Mamaw. I feel much better now. I'm so glad you were here tonight."

She kissed my forehead. "God's timing is always perfect."

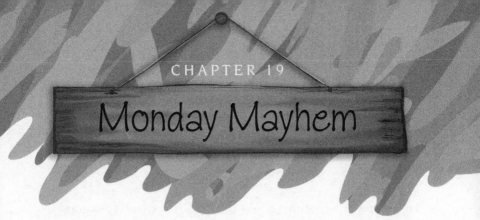

CHAPTER 19

Monday Mayhem

Lola didn't show up for church on Sunday. Aunt Janie said Madison's party went a little later than planned. And then Lola slept the rest of the day away, so I didn't get to talk to her at all.

God must have known I needed the time to regain my perspective, because by the end of Sunday, I felt energized, and ready to start a new week.

On Monday, I jumped out of bed an hour early, which startled Kendall, who jammed her pillow over her head.

"Allie, when is your new house going to be ready?"

"Oh, come on! I'm not that bad as a roommate. Who are you gonna get to sing with you when I'm gone?" I began to hum one of Kendall's new melodies.

Kendall sat up. "You're chipper this morning."

"Well," I began smoothing my blankets on my bed and choosing my outfit for the day. "We have a steering committee meeting today after school, so I'm hoping we'll get some things back on track. I'm focusing on giving all my cares and worries to God."

"But first there's school," Kendall said. "And Mr. Vicker told us that we actually have to work this week."

I turned and pushed my hands out from both sides of my face, forming a tunnel that pointed toward Kendall. "Focus, Kendall. 1 Peter 5:7."

She yawned, stretched, and finally managed to stand. "Gotcha. Hey, maybe I'll get paired with Parker for the science project."

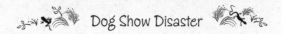

I sighed and shook my head. "You are shameless."

"And now that I'm up, I'm also hungry. I hope Hunter hasn't eaten all the cereal."

It was my mom's turn to take us all to school, and I wanted to sit by Lola, so I jumped in the back seat of the SUV instead of riding my normal shotgun.

"You sit up front," I said to Hunter

"Cool!" Hunter jumped up in his seat and held up his cardboard tube. "Made some more adjustments to the Dimple-Dunk 5000. We almost had to change the name to the Dimple-Dunk 6000!"

"What are you talking about, Hunter?" Mom asked.

"It's a plan to bring in money for the animal shelter. Lots of it! Can I present my idea to the committee today, Allie? Mr. Dimple needs the go-ahead soon so he can start building."

"Let me see what's on Miss Lewis's agenda when I get to school, and I'll let you know."

We pulled up to Ruby and Lola's house, and I gestured to Lola to sit by me in the way back.

"So, how was the party?"

Lola slouched, and ran her hand through the pink streak in her hair. "It was all right."

"All right? That's all?"

Lola settled in and buckled her seatbelt. "Pretty much. The girls were nice. We played games, ate a bunch of junk food, sang karaoke, and danced."

I stared her down.

"Oh, yeah, and we gave each other manicures." Lola held up her hands to show me her magenta-colored nails. "See?"

"Okay, so did you take any pictures of Madison's room? I'm dying to see what they did after they knocked the wall out."

"Yeah, I did. I remembered right before the party was over and I asked Madison if she could give me a tour of the house. She was happy to let me take pictures. Wanna see?"

Lola wiggled her eyebrows up and down, and pulled the phone out of her jacket pocket.

"Of course, I want to see!"

Lola poked her screen and frowned. "What are *these* pictures?"

She scrolled and then showed me about twenty selfies of the girls I met by the pool on Saturday.

"Those sneaky girls," Lola said. "They must have gotten a hold of my phone. I thought I lost it Saturday night, but then Veronica said she found it under a pillow in the morning. They must have had it that whole time, taking selfies."

"No wonder you didn't return my texts."

"You should really put a password on your phone, Lola," Ruby said.

"I guess so. But no one's ever messed with it before."

Lola scrolled past the selfies and finally got to a couple of pictures of Madison's room. I gasped. It looked a lot like the room Kendall and I stayed in at the movie star home in Hollywood a few months ago. White quilt, white lace curtains, and a coffee table.

A coffee table—in a girl's room.

"Well, she wasn't kidding when she said she made improvements. It's beautiful."

Lola shrugged. "It's fancy, and I like all the style and detail, but it lacks the coziness and charm it used to have when you lived there."

"And clutter," Kendall added.

"Okay, I'll take that as a compliment—from both of you." I

stared closer at the picture. "Where's all her *stuff*? Doesn't she have any books? Stuffed animals? Souvenirs? This looks like a hotel room."

"Uh, she has a huge walk-in closet," Lola said. "But I mostly saw clothes in there, so who knows?"

"Did you see Parker?" Kendall asked.

I rolled my eyes at her.

"No. Madison banished Parker and her dad to the game room. I heard some bomb blasts throughout the night. Madison said they planned to watch guy movies and eat stacks of pizzas."

"That's what I would do," Hunter said.

"And did she like her gift?"

Lola reached up to touch the matching necklace she had on. "Yes. And she wanted us both to wear them today. I'm not really into doing the twin thing, but it seemed like it meant a lot to her."

"I meant the Bible verse. Did she like that?"

"She didn't really say. But it doesn't matter. I just pray she'll keep it and that it will encourage her. She's been going through a lot, with the divorce and the move and all."

I love Lola's heart.

Hmmm. Maybe I've been a little harsh, calling Madison "Mad-girl."

"Did you know that Madison's mom is a clothes model?"

"Really?" I hadn't ever given a thought to Madison's mom before. "That must be why she's drawn to you, then. You could be a model."

"Madison said that's why she lives with her dad, because her mom travels so much. But I guess she's taking Madison to Paris for the whole summer. It's practically all she could talk about all night."

"Is Parker going too?"

Ruby pointed her thumb at Kendall. "Does she have a crush, or what?"

"Ya think?" I bopped Kendall in the back of the head.

"Parker's *not* going," Hunter added from the front seat. "He said that would be *the* most boring thing he could think to do in the summer. He's stayin' here and we're gonna hang out and explore the woods together."

Kendall sighed. "Oh, good."

When we pulled into the parking lot of the school, Madison was waiting on the curb. She was wearing another flowery dress—this one purple with pink flowers all over. And, of course, bracelets.

"Hi, Lola. I wore my necklace." She pulled it away from her neck with both thumbs. "I really, really love it." Madison ignored every other person who piled out of the SUV.

"I'm glad," Lola said.

"Do you want to walk to class together? I'll show you some of the pictures we took at the party." Madison turned toward the quad and took her phone out of her backpack.

"Yeah," Lola said. "And I have some photos to show you too." They walked away, toward the dreaded room 220—to brave a whole Monday with Miss Lewis.

I spent every free moment that morning working on Bark Fest details. Mr. Vicker didn't make it very easy with all the work he was assigning. By lunch, I felt like I needed to go to the library and work some more, instead of hanging out with my cousins, so I'd be ready for the long meeting after school. The more I worked on the carnival details, the more excited I got about the whole thing. This Bark Fest really was a good idea! At one point, I took my phone out to check Madison's funding page. It still read the same as before—promising the winner an appearance on her dad's show—and the donations were up to five-thousand dollars!

Lord, please help me know what to do about this. I'm giving this worry to you. Madison's the fundraising chairperson, so help me to focus on the other stuff.

I dialed the animal shelter, and Mr. Felix answered.

"Hello, Mr. Felix? This is Allie Carroway . . . Yes, I know . . . The Bark Fest is going to be great . . . that sounds wonderful . . . I'm sure Mr. Dimple could help you design plans for all those upgrades. Mr. Felix, I was wondering if you reserved the Kiroli dog park for the 15th . . . You did? That's great! Okay, then I'm going to have some flyers made up and get those handed out to all the kids at our school . . . Yes, I'm very excited. Also, do you think your employees would be willing to be judges for the dog show? . . . Awesome. Thanks, Mr. Felix. . . . You, too. Bye."

I sat there at the little table in the deserted library and took in a deep breath.

So far, so good.

I finished up my school day with choir and math. Mr. Vicker brought his boards, and I got to kick one. It had been such a productive day that by the time the bell rang, I was ready to stroll into that steering committee meeting and grab the wheel.

On my way over, Lola stopped me. She looked white as a marshmallow.

"Allie, I have to talk to you. Something's up."

I took my heavy backpack off and set it on the ground.

"What's going on, Lola? Are you sick?"

She grabbed her stomach, and looked down at the ground. She breathed in, blew it out, and then looked up at the clouds. Her eyes filled with tears.

I was sure someone had died, or was on their way to being dead.

I grabbed her by both shoulders. "What? It's okay, you can tell me."

Lola started all-out crying then. I picked up my backpack and led her to a table in the quad.

We sat there for a few minutes. Lola was inconsolable. Where were the other cousins? I was going to have to leave for my meeting soon.

Finally, Lola looked up at me and spoke. "Allie, your skit is on the Internet."

She might as well have been speaking French, because what she said made no sense.

"What are you talking about? What skit?"

"The one from Comedy Night. The Lewis-Beetle skit. It's online. And there's already been tons of hits and shares and comments, and people are so upset . . ."

"The Lewis-Beetle skit? You mean the one I did for our family? You must be mistaken. No one would put that online. It was private."

Lola just looked at me and wiped her nose with a napkin that had been left on the table.

My heart began pounding faster and faster. This couldn't be true, could it? The only one who videoed that silly skit was Lola.

"Lola, I know you wouldn't post that video, so it can't be online. I mean—how could that happen?"

Lola took out her phone, sniffed some more, and pulled up her FriendClips app. She opened to a girl's page named "Frenelope." Then I saw it. A post titled "SPM mocks FPM. Can she be trusted?" There was a video attached, and the start screen showed a picture of me, standing in my Aunt Kassie and

Uncle Wayne's living room, about to begin my Lewis-Beetle performance. A start arrow covered my face.

"Do I dare click this?" I asked Lola. "Is the *whole* skit on this video?"

Lola nodded and her shoulders heaved up and down.

I clicked, and watched in horror as I detailed the flaws of Miss Lewis—our Faculty Project Manager—and then I got hit in the face with the pie.

It was the hilarious turned horrific. Out there for all to see.

One thousand ninety-one views so far. And 541 comments.

"Who is this Frenelope? And how did *she* get this video?"

All Lola could do was shake her head and cry.

But then I knew.

The party. The "lost" phone.

Mix that with a trusting cousin and a bully in the bayou who wanted to see me drown.

I *should have kept my eyes open wider, Mamaw.*

"Allie! There you are!" Ruby came running over. "Have you seen . . ."

I put my hand up to stop her words. She froze and put a hand over her mouth when she saw her sister drowning in a puddle of tears.

"Did they steal the video from your phone, sis?"

Lola didn't say anything.

"Oh, no! How can anyone be so cruel?" She sat down next to Lola and put her arm around her shoulders.

Kendall was next to arrive. She looked around at the messy scene. "Everyone's seen it. I can't believe this is happening. Just like wildfire and peanut butter."

"Can we take it off?" Ruby asked. "Is there a way to delete it before it spreads anymore?" She scrolled on her phone and poked the screen a couple of times. "I don't know how to do that, do you, Allie?"

I shook my head, and in the distance, I saw Miss Lewis heading to the library.

I looked at the time on my phone. Steering committee meeting in ten minutes.

God, help!

I stood, and straightened myself up. "Okay, I have to go to a meeting." I put my hand on Lola's back. "Lola, I know you would never do anything to hurt anyone—especially me."

Lola looked up and wiped some more tears with the soggy napkin.

"On your way home, try to find out if there is a way to delete the video. Maybe we can figure out who this Frenelope is and ask her to please take it down. I bet it's a fake account started by one of the girls at the party. Until we figure it out, we'll just have to pray that it all dies down."

"Do you think Miss Lewis knows about it yet?" Kendall asked.

I glanced toward the library. "I bet she doesn't. She's all business. Probably doesn't have time or interest in social media."

"I hope you're right," Ruby said.

Me too.

CHAPTER 20

Burgers and Indigestion

My outlook on the meeting had changed in an instant. I was no longer looking to grab the wheel. Now I just hoped to buckle my seatbelt and hang on for dear life.

When I entered the library, there sat Madison, Samara, and Ronnie. There were a few other kids too—recruits we were supposed to bring on this day. Miss Lewis had her back to me—making some copies on the machine in the corner.

My classmates stared at me as I approached the table. Had they seen the video? Then I noticed all their phones sitting on the table, among the spiral notebooks and pencils.

Yes, of course they had seen it.

Miss Lewis turned and walked back to the table with the copies. "Carroway, I'm glad you're finally here so we can get started."

Madison held a post-it note up in my direction. It said "Lewis-Beetle" and there was an arrow pointing toward Miss Lewis. She smirked and then she crumpled it up and shoved it in her backpack.

Miss Lewis sat down. "Burgers will be here in an hour. Let's get started. Do we have a report from our SPM?" Miss Lewis folded her hands on her pile of notes and turned toward me. I was not ready to give a report now. The only thing I wanted to do was throw up my lunch.

Just then, the library door squeaked open and in ran Hunter.

"Sorry I'm late! Allie, did you tell them my idea yet?"

Madison flipped her hair. "Hunter, we're in an important meeting."

Hunter pushed his glasses up on his nose. "I know. That's why I'm here. I have plans that can bring in thousands of dollars—I'm sure of it."

Madison harrumphed. Miss Lewis rose from her chair and addressed Hunter. I think I saw her grin with her eyes.

"Come on over. We were just getting started with Miss Carroway's reports, so if she's fine with it, you may speak."

Thank the Lord for Hunter. His enthusiasm and timing are impeccable.

"Go ahead, cousin."

Hunter sat down in Miss Lewis's space, popped the end off his cardboard tube, and pulled out the rolled-up plans. "Thanks," he said, and then he grinned that famous grin.

It even made me feel better for a moment.

The Dimple-Dunk 5000 was a go. Hunter's eyes gleamed as he addressed the group. "I'll have Mr. Dimple begin assembly ASAP. And you can figure out how you want to nominate and then vote for the people who can bring in the most dunking money. Now if you'll excuse me, my ride is waiting."

Hunter gathered up his plans, slid them back in the cardboard tube, and sprinted out. He looked like one of those track runners carrying a baton. I wanted to dart out with him, go hide in the Lickety Split, and not come out until all this FriendClips mess had blown over.

If it ever would.

"Miss Carroway, are you ready to give your report now?" Miss Lewis peeked over her reading glasses at me. I tapped my pencil on the table and considered my next move. The best thing to do was to act enthusiastic and competent. And don't say "um."

"Yes, ma'am, I have a lot to report." I began by listing all the vendors I had hired, and ended with the fun report about the dog trick clinic that would be put on by Mr. Felix at Kiroli Park on April 15th. The kids in the room all perked up and began talking about their dogs and what they would like to teach them. Madison remained quiet, and glared at me.

Her report was next, and it was all I could do to hold my lips together when she mentioned her funding page and all the money it was generating. Ronnie then reported that he already had enough volunteers to staff all the game booths all day long. I guess he wasn't kidding when he said he was good at recruiting.

Samara James reported that the mural was already halfway done, and she showed us samples of logos she had created. We voted unanimously to approve the use of one of them, and Samara gave me a thumb drive with the design on it so I could add it to my dog trick clinic flyers.

Before we knew it, the burgers had been delivered, and Miss Lewis called a fifteen-minute break for us to eat.

That would not have been my choice, because as soon as she called break, everyone picked up their phones, including Miss Lewis!

I had to keep her from seeing that video, so I edged my way over to talk to her.

"I'm excited about all the great reports," I said. "Is there anything you think we're missing?"

Miss Lewis scrolled on her phone and ignored me.

"Miss Lewis?"

She frowned.

"Carroway, we're on a break. I appreciate your diligence, but I need a moment here."

"Oh. I'm sorry, ma'am."

Miss Lewis sighed. "I'm sorry for snapping at you. I'm just waiting on a text from Mrs. Mellon. Little Bethany had a setback today. They think she might be bleeding on her brain. If that's the case, she's in real danger."

"Oh, no, that's terrible." This day was just getting worse.

"When we get caught up on all of this carnival planning, let's talk with the steering committee about a way we can help the Mellon family, okay?"

"Sure."

She set her phone down. "I have to run to my classroom for just a minute, and when I return let's resume so we can get out of here faster."

She walked out the door. Everything was silent, except for the sound of one phone—held by Ronnie Alexander—over in the corner of the library. A few kids were gathered around the screen, watching with their surprised eyes and mouths open.

The familiar words were mine.

I'd like to tell you a story about a pest that is taking over Louisiana . . .

Miss Lewis returned, right at the part where I get hit with the pie.

"Miss Lewis, did you know you were on the Internet?" Madison asked.

Miss Lewis looked me straight in the eyes. "Yes, I did. Now let's resume our meeting. We have a carnival to plan."

CHAPTER 21

Fire Storm

I used to think that nothing would be scarier than having a wildfire rage through my neighborhood. But during the next two weeks, I learned that having people blast you on social media is worse. At least with a fire, you have a warning. You can escape. You can put it out. And people who don't even know you try to *help*.

But that wasn't so with my little Lewis-Beetle video. I told my parents about it the first day it appeared online, and while we managed to get the first post erased, by then it had been shared and copied, and the thing went viral. Fires burned throughout cyberspace, and it seemed that everyone—at school, in the community, in the state of Louisiana, worldwide, and possibly aliens on Mars—had something to say about it.

"Check this out, Mom." I sat on the barstool pulled up to the kitchen island, eating breakfast, and reading comments from one of the posts. "Allie Carroway and her family are phonies! They should be ashamed of this display of disrespect, and their show should be cancelled immediately."

Mom walked over and pulled the phone out of my hand. "I'll be holding on to this—until you promise not to read any more comments."

"Aww, come on. There are some good ones too. I like the ones that defend me."

That's about one in fifty, though.

Mom tossed my phone in the junk drawer and came back to sit down next to me.

"Allie Kate, I want you to listen carefully. Those people commenting on the Internet don't know you, and they certainly don't care about you. Because *if* they did, they wouldn't be able to comment at all, because they would *know* that you're a caring and loving girl, and that you didn't mean to disrespect your teacher. Now, was the skit totally appropriate? No. Should you apologize to Miss Lewis? Probably. But they have no right to disrespect you—someone they don't even know—in such a public way. It's disgraceful. *They're* doing the very thing that they accuse *you* of doing."

Mom got up and started aggressively wiping down the kitchen island counter.

Then she threw the rag down in the sink and supported herself with her hands.

"And another thing. Don't let your enemies convince you that you're someone you're not. They want you to believe that you're a loser, but you are God's beautiful daughter—case closed! God says that 'he who began a good work in you will be faithful to complete it.' We've all got flaws, Allie, and if that weren't true, we wouldn't need a savior."

She picked up the rag and wiped the same counter again, threw it down, and stormed out to the living room. She hit her knees by the couch and started praying silently.

My mom prays when she gets fighting mad.

And the praying worked for me at that moment, because suddenly I felt the confidence to go out and face another school day, where I was sure there would be more nasty glances, whispering, and rumors that some of the kids wanted me removed from my position as Student Project Manager.

At least the next day was the dog-training clinic at Kiroli Park. We had 175 dogs and their owners signed up to attend the half-day event. No one seemed to have a bad comment about that.

CHAPTER 22

No Show

The steering committee, my cousins, and I arrived at the Kiroli Dog Park Saturday morning at 7:30 am—ninety minutes early. We had purchased donuts, pastries, fruit, and orange juice, and we mixed up several five-gallon jugs of iced tea for the participants. We also provided a treat bar for the dogs.

"These look good enough for *me* to eat," Hunter said as he spread the dog treats out on the picnic table. He held one up to his mouth that looked like a chocolate bone dipped at the ends in white chocolate. "Do you dare me?"

"Of course, I dare you!" Kendall said.

Not surprisingly, Hunter took a nibble. He grimaced, then chewed, and swallowed. "Not bad," he said. "But I think I'll save the rest for T-Rex."

T-Rex was already in the dog park, hanging out with all the other Carroway dogs, being "dog-sat" by our Uncle Saul. I glanced over and saw a Frisbee fly, and I thought I saw Ruby's dog Max jump up to catch it in his mouth.

"Hey, Ruby, looks like Max could be a competitor in the Spectacular Dog Trick contest."

"I hope so. I've been working with him. All the research I've been doing about dog shows has inspired me."

Ruby was doing a great job organizing everything having to do with the dog show. In fact, all my cousins had really rallied around me that last two weeks. It had been especially encouraging to me after the day when Ronnie Alexander informed me that forty of his volunteers were dropping out of the carnival.

"Allie, they say they don't want to do it now if the Carroways are involved. I'm sorry."

That had been painful, and I had to work to hold back tears as I talked to Ronnie.

Miss Lewis, who had been talking to my aunts and mom, came over to where we were setting up the dog treats. She took a deep breath and . . . she smiled!

It was a really teeny-tiny one, but still!

"Carroway, are you ready for this? One hundred seventy-five dogs? Can you believe what we've been able to pull off in such a short amount of time?"

I still couldn't believe that she was talking to me—after that dumb Lewis-Beetle skit hit the Internet. In fact, she had never even mentioned it, and that sort of made me nervous.

I checked my sports watch. "We're ready early—that's good. Mr. Felix should be here in a few minutes, and he'll let us know how he wants us to organize things with the dogs. This is going to be like a Pre-Bark Fest!"

"I brought my dog," Miss Lewis said. "She's in the car."

"You have a dog?" Kendall asked.

"Of course," Miss Lewis said. "Her name's Daisy, and she's a Catahoula Cur. She's a great hunting dog. Come meet her."

A *Catahoula. And Miss Lewis hunts too? Cool.*

On the way over to Miss Lewis's car—this time she brought a Jeep—my cousins and I ran into Madison Doonsberry. Lola immediately walked away, her heart still broken from the way she was deceived by Madison's friends at the party.

"Allie, *please* tell Lola that I had nothing to do with that video being taken off her phone. I've disowned my friends, and I'm sorry as I can be. I don't know what else I can do."

It was a pathetic explanation, and I wasn't buying it *at all*.

This is me—Allie Carroway—keeping my eyes wide open, you little bully.

"Where's *your* dog, Madison?" Hunter asked, innocently enough.

Madison frowned. "Parker's bringing him in a few minutes. Chief could win best-looking dog."

I had to admit, the girl was a quick thinker. Chief was Parker's dog—a tan and black "King" German Shepherd, and he was almost as big as Parker.

I think I was the only one of the cousins who knew what had happened to Madison's dog.

"Daisy, meet the kids." Miss Lewis interrupted our Madison circle, bringing Daisy in on a leash. She was cute, in a unique kind of way. She was white, with tan legs, and her body and head had big black spots, and then a bunch of little black spots. Kind of like freckles.

"A leopard dog!" Hunter said. "I love these." He reached down to pet Daisy. "You wanna go meet T-Rex? He'll love having a leopard dog for a friend."

Miss Lewis grinned with her eyes. "Yes, let's go on over. I see we have some dogs and owners arriving. What time did you say Mr. Felix was coming?"

"He was supposed to arrive at 8:00."

It was 8:45.

"If I were you, I'd give him a call."

My stomach ached a little as I ran over to the covered pavilion to make the call to Mr. Felix.

This is not a good day for car trouble, God.

The phone rang sixteen times. Finally, Mr. Felix answered.

"Well, hello, Allie! How are you on this lovely Louisiana morning?"

Hmmm. He sounds fine.

"I'm great, sir. I was wondering if everything is okay with you, though. We have dogs and owners arriving here at the dog park, and I thought we had agreed for you to arrive at 8:00."

There was a moment of silence on the other end.

Finally, Mr. Felix spoke. "What do you mean? I thought you wanted to reschedule the clinic for next week. My secretary left me a note that you had called . . ."

I almost dropped my phone. "Oh, no, sir! I never asked to reschedule. We're having it this morning." I looked down at my watch and then over at the huge, barking crowd that was gathering by the dog park gate. "In about fifteen minutes!"

"Oh, dear, well I don't understand what happened. My secretary made it clear that you had called and rescheduled for next week."

"Well, whatever happened was a mistake! Mr. Felix, can you still come and do it this morning?"

More silence.

"Allie, I would if I could, but I'm in New Orleans."

I wanted to lie down on the picnic bench and die. "Okay, thank you, Mr. Felix."

"I'm very sorry, Allie. Are we still on for next week?"

"Sure."

If anyone shows up. If I decide to show up.

"Allie, why are you laying on the top of the picnic table?"

Lola. Her eyes were red and watery.

I sat up. "Mr. Felix isn't coming. Someone called the office this week, and told him I wanted to reschedule the clinic for next week."

She nodded. "Let me guess. Was it Veronica, Chloe, Kaitlyn, Penny, or was it Madison, the ringleader, herself?"

I narrowed my eyes. "I don't know, but I'll find out."

Miss Lewis jogged over with Daisy. "So where's our dog trainer?"

"He's not coming," I said. "Someone called and claimed that I wanted it rescheduled. And now he's in New Orleans, so I guess this isn't happening today."

Miss Lewis joined me, sitting cross-legged on top of the table. "Wow."

She sighed and thought for a moment, chin in her hands.

"Well, at least they got some tasty snacks." She turned to look at me. "You better go break the news, Carroway."

I pointed a thumb to my chest. "You want *me* to go?"

"Yes. Leaders must be able to stand the heat. But I'll be right there next to you, and if they charge, we can use Parker's dog as a shield. That thing is huge."

That made me laugh. But I still didn't want to go.

"I'll come too, Allie, and I'll stand right next to you."

"Thanks, Lola."

The three of us walked toward the crowd of kids, parents, and dogs. People were already checking their watches, and I could hear comments about things starting late as I grabbed the bullhorn from the sign-in table and flipped the on switch.

Here goes. I'm doomed.

I tried not to shake, but it didn't work. That bullhorn was wobbling all over.

"Ladies and gentlemen . . . and dogs . . . our trainer is not able to make it today. I am sorry for the inconvenience. I was just on the phone with him, and we have rescheduled our clinic for next Saturday, same time, right here."

People shook their heads. Kids stomped away. Dogs howled—
it sounded like even they were complaining.

"We'll have more dog treats, and possibly breakfast burritos . . . thank you for your understanding."

I flipped the bullhorn to off. A little girl came up to me and
tugged on my T-shirt.

"Are we gonna see the doggies do twicks?"

I started to shake my head, when I heard Uncle Saul
approaching.

"Frisbee clinic! I'm an expert on teaching dogs to catch!
See me over at the chain link in five minutes!"

The little girl's eyes brightened. "Let's go, Mommy!"

Good old Uncle Saul.

What would I do without my family?

About a third of the people stayed for the frisbee clinic.
Others left right after my announcement. A couple of people
came up to encourage me, but I also overheard some other
kinds of comments.

"I am *not* packing you kids up and coming again next week,
that's for sure."

"What's with the Carroways lately? Untrustworthy!"

"What a disorganized mess."

And, the worst comment came from the center of a group
of OMS students as they walked to the cars with their dogs:

"I can't believe I voted for her. What was I thinking?"

CHAPTER 23

Prayers and Petitions

By the time I got home, I was fighting mad. I pulled up my FriendClips account and clicked on the settings button, changing my private account to public. Then I typed out these words:

MADISON DOONSBERRY IS A LIAR AND A CHEAT AND A FAKE.

She stole my cousin's phone, and downloaded a video that was supposed to be private. She also didn't get permission from her dad to offer the winner of the fundraising drawing a part on his show, so she has cheated all of you too!!!!!!!!!

I tagged everyone from the steering committee and the OMS Eagles page, so that anyone who followed that would see my post. Now *everyone* would know about this awful girl.

My index finger hovered over the "post" button.

And then my mom's words came back to me.

"They're doing the very thing that they accuse you of doing."

And . . .

"We've all got flaws, Allie, and if that weren't true, we wouldn't need a savior."

I put the phone down on the table. Stared at the words that had spewed out of my heart and onto the screen. They were angry, harsh, bitter words. Written about another girl, who was created by God, who had flaws, just like me.

I can fight better than this, Lord.

I picked up my phone and deleted the post. Then I threw the phone in the kitchen junk drawer and ran out to the Lickety Split, where I hit my knees, so I could just be still—and pray.

God, you can have this whole thing. The carnival. The dog show. The humiliation from the viral video. The failed dog clinic. Madison hating me. I can't deal with any of it! I'm just a kid, and I'm in way over my head. I don't know what to do.

I kneeled there for what seemed like forever. Then, when my knees finally turned numb, I lay down on the beanbag and stared up at the 1 Peter 5:7 Scripture board above my head again. This time, a different part of the verse popped out at me.

"*. . . He cares about you.*"

On Monday, everyone at school was quiet about the no-show at the dog park. I did notice lots of shifty glances coming my way during lunch, so I figured they had to be talking, but hey—as long as it didn't end up on the Internet, I considered that a win.

But then, "Terrible Tuesday" arrived. During our morning nutrition break, Lola sent me a text with some pictures attached.

This is going around in our class right now.

I clicked on the first picture and then enlarged it so I could read the words:

Petition to Remove Student Project Manager
We, the students of Ouachita Middle School, hereby request that Allie Carroway be removed from her position as Student Project Manager for the year-end project. Since she took over the position, volunteers have with-

drawn, events have been canceled, and negative publicity for the school has been generated by an inappropriate video that was posted on social media. We feel it is in the best interest of Ouachita Middle School and the West Monroe Animal Shelter for this action to be taken immediately, and that the second student in charge—Madison Doonsberry—be appointed Student Project Manager.

The petition demands were hard enough to read. The *torture* was reading names of my friends who had already signed it! I clicked on the picture of the next page, and there were 150 signatures.

Another text buzzed in from Lola.

> Don't worry, I didn't sign it.

And she put a happy face emoji on the end of that text. I texted her back.

> You're the best.

She buzzed back.

> What are you going to do?

I thought a minute.
What should I do, God?
A calm settled over me, and I knew exactly what to text back to Lola.

> Wait to see what they do with it.

There wasn't really anything else I could do. I knew Madison wasn't the right person for the job. Right now, she was working on handing the school a lawsuit that could air on *Lunker Law*. I checked her funding page. Six-thousand dollars raised.

By the end of the week, three quarters of the student body had signed the petition. And on the day of the rescheduled dog clinic, only thirty kids and their dogs showed up. But everyone who came loved the special attention they received from Mr. Felix, and they took home extra breakfast burritos and dog treats.

I had a lump in my throat the entire time. Thankfully, Madison didn't show up, or I might have pounced on her and wrestled her into the creek.

I sat on a swing on the nearby playground, watching the last of the dog owners thanking Mr. Felix. Miss Lewis brought her cute dog Daisy over on a leash, and she sat down on the swing next to me.

"That could have been much worse, Carroway."

I dug my toes in the dirt as I swung a little. "Yeah. Too bad people stayed home. They missed something really special."

I reached out to pet Daisy, and wished Hazel Mae were here. I guess I hadn't shown much enthusiasm either—leaving my own dog at home.

"I talked to Christie—I mean, Mrs. Mellon—today. Bethany's doing a little better."

I perked up. "That's great news."

"She's coming to my classroom Monday after school. We'd both like to meet with you. It's important. Can you be there? 1600 hours?"

I gulped. "Sure. What time is that, exactly?"

"Four o'clock."

"Yeah, I'll be there."

CHAPTER 24

Resignation

Dear Miss Lewis,

To ensure the success of the Ouachita Middle School year-end project, I feel it is necessary to resign my position as Student Project Manager. I regret that things did not go more smoothly under my leadership, and I promise to do everything I can to support you and the new Student Project Manager from this point forward. Thank you for giving me a chance to serve.

Sincerely,
Allie Carroway

Miss Lewis and Mrs. Mellon sat across the desk from me in room 220. They took turns reading my letter silently, and then they placed it on the desk—right next to the "Petition to Remove Allie Carroway as Student Project Manager."

"This must have been difficult for you to write," Miss Lewis said.

I nodded. "Yes, ma'am."

Mrs. Mellon picked up the petition, and turned it to face me on the desk. "Did you, by any chance, know about *this* when you wrote your letter?"

I swallowed hard, bit my bottom lip, and nodded. "I've

known about that for a week." I reached for the petition and flipped through the pages. "That's a lot of signatures."

My eyes filled up with water.

Don't blink, Allie. Don't let the tears fall.

"I did my best."

"I know." Mrs. Mellon reached out and patted my hand.

"Do you think you did anything wrong?" Miss Lewis asked.

I thought a minute. The answer was no—except for one thing.

"I shouldn't have made fun of you. I'm very sorry."

Miss Lewis cocked her head and looked confused. "What are you talking about?"

Is it possible she didn't know about the video?

I took a deep breath. "I performed a goofy skit at my family's comedy night that went viral on the Internet. It was about you, and I shouldn't have done it." I looked down at the floor. "I'm so sorry, Miss Lewis. Will you forgive me?"

"For the Lewis-Beetle skit?" Miss Lewis was grinning now. "I thought it was hilarious."

Both Miss Lewis and Mrs. Mellon were giggling a little. Miss Lewis—giggling!

I picked my head up. "You did?"

"Of course. I messaged it to all my friends and family." Miss Lewis leaned forward. "Allie, has that been bothering you all this time?"

She called me Allie.

I finally lost a tear and had to wipe it from my cheek. "That's what's been bothering me the most! My cousin recorded that video. She never meant for it to get out. Some girls at a party stole her phone, downloaded, and posted it. Things went viral, and now it seems everyone has turned against me."

"Hmmmm." Miss Lewis tapped her fingers on the desk.

"That doesn't make sense. I would think the kids would love you even more after that video. I know I'm not everyone's favorite."

Mrs. Mellon nodded. "Sounds like a smear campaign to me."

I sniffed. "Smear campaign?"

Miss Lewis picked up the petition and flipped through the pages. "Yes. It seems that someone is working hard to get you removed from this project. Do you have any idea who it could be?"

Yes.

"No, ma'am. I mean—I have some ideas, but no proof."

"Any idea who called and cancelled the dog trainer? Because I know it wasn't you."

Well, that's a relief.

"Once again—I have ideas, but no proof."

"Carroway, stay right here. We'll be right back."

Whatever you say, Miss Lewis. I'll even do push-ups if you want me to.

Both teachers got up and walked out the door. I turned my head and could see them talking through the window. Miss Lewis had her arms crossed, and Mrs. Mellon had one hand on her hip and one on her forehead.

Finally, Miss Lewis walked back in the classroom—alone.

"Is Mrs. Mellon all right?" I was so wrapped up in my own problems that I hadn't even asked her how she was feeling.

"Christie's fine. But she had to go meet with a specialist about Bethany's eyes. I guess she may have major problems with her vision now. That poor little girl."

Miss Lewis picked up my resignation letter.

"I appreciate your thoughtfulness in drafting this letter, Allie. It proves to me that you have the well-being of the school foremost on your heart."

She picked up the petition and scanned it, then looked

at me. "Madison Doonsberry, huh? That's who they want to lead them?"

I nodded. "Yes, ma'am. I suppose we should give them what they want."

Miss Lewis took my letter and placed it on top of the petition. Then she turned both documents sideways, and began to rip them to pieces!

My jaw felt like it hit the floor, and my throat dropped into my stomach. I'm pretty sure my eyes popped out for a second too.

Miss Lewis continued to rip, then she walked over to the trashcan in the corner of the classroom and threw the shreds in. She strode back, pressed her lips together, and breathed deep through her nose.

"Well, they're not going to get what they *want*. They're going to get what they *need*. And that's you, Carroway. *You're* going to continue as Student Project Manager, because I believe you're the right person for the job. It may be a dog show disaster right now, but this thing is going to turn around, you'll see."

I shot to my feet. I didn't know whether to jump up and down and cheer, or jump up and down and protest. The only thing I actually did was pound my fist on the desk.

Miss Lewis raised one eyebrow.

I put my hand over my mouth. "I'm sorry. I'm just . . . I don't know. I really appreciate you standing by me."

Miss Lewis pounded the desk too. "No, that's good! I'm glad you have a little fight left in you."

Miss Lewis sat back down. "Plus, it's an honor to stand by you and finish this project. I understand how it feels not to be the popular one at this school."

I hung my head. "I'm really sorry about that too."

Miss Lewis shrugged. "I'm used to it. Hey—I'm not ashamed

to demand excellence. It's my job to shape my students and challenge them—not to be their friend. I know—I can be over-the-top intense, and that doesn't help—but it's my personality. And I know kids joke that I never smile, but do you want to know when I smile, Carroway? I smile when I see a kid like your brother get into college and study engineering. Someday he'll invent something that will change the world, and I'd like to think I pushed him to try something better than pranking all the time."

I smiled. "That makes a lot of sense."

"So . . ." Miss Lewis stood up and walked me to the door. "Are we going to stick this thing out together—work as hard as we can, and let the outcome speak for itself?" She held out a fist.

I met it with my fist. "Sure. Let's do it."

Miss Lewis opened the door for me. "You know, we *could* use this unpopular team thing to our advantage."

"Really? How?"

Miss Lewis tapped her temple with her index finger. "Oh no—I'm not going to do your thinking for you, Carroway. You're a leader. Act like one."

CHAPTER 25

Mother's Day

The pep talk and fist bump from Miss Lewis energized me. The first thing I did when I got home was text all the steering committee and call a meeting for the next day. At the meeting, I apologized for making such a silly video and for letting it get out on the Internet to embarrass the school. I also apologized for not confirming the dates with Mr. Felix on the Friday before the first dog training. I suggested that we schedule one more dog training clinic, and then I asked them if they would consider showing some enthusiasm so that the kids of the school would come out. I also assured them that for the next month I would focus on getting all our volunteers back, and I told them how much I noticed and appreciated all their hard work.

I even said that to Madison. After all, her funding page was now up to seven-thousand dollars, and I *did* notice that she was working hard—even if it was to embarrass me and bankrupt the school.

When she scowled back at me, I ignored it.

This scowling and ignoring continued at meetings and during school for the next couple of weeks.

Finally, after what seemed like hours of Lickety-Split prayer time and God telling me to finally admit *my* part in the mess, I decided to be obedient and pull her aside after a meeting in Miss Lewis's room.

"Madison, can you hang out here for a minute?"

Madison steamed. "What do you want?" She slammed her backpack down on the chair.

I dropped my arms to my sides with hands open, asked God for super-strength, and then spoke.

"I just want to say that if I've done *anything* to offend you, I'm sorry. I didn't realize it till recently, but I really miss my old house, and now *you* live there, so I've been mad at you, and I know that's not your fault. Will you please forgive me?"

Madison said nothing. Just stared down at her backpack.

This isn't going so great, God.

"Anyway, I hope we can start over, and be friends someday."

Madison finally turned to face me with her hands on her hips, but she didn't make eye contact.

"Thank you. I'll think about it."

And she turned and walked out the door.

I didn't talk much more to Madison again until Mother's Day—in the bathroom at The Cracker Barrel.

Mamaw had been recovering from a cold all week, so—though she protested—we insisted she not cook.

"We're taking the moms out," Dad said.

And The Cracker Barrel restaurant won the vote for best place to go, because of its delicious gravy, rocking chairs, and checker games.

When we all piled into the lobby, I thought the young hostess was going to flip out.

"Carroways? You're coming to *our* restaurant?" She looked beyond us kids to count heads. "Uh, do you have a reservation? It's Mother's Day, and we're kinda busy . . ."

The manager—Martha, who's my mom's friend from high school—came to her rescue.

"We have some tables set up for them in the side room, Charlotte."

Charlotte breathed a sigh and put a hand on her chest. "Oh, thank heavens. I didn't know how I was going to turn away the Carroways."

She led us past full tables filled with families and over to the side room. It was a large space separated from the main restaurant by a half-wall, and it held just enough tables and chairs for our huge group.

At first, all us cousins clustered together at the same table, but then were reprimanded by my Uncle Wayne.

"Sit by your moms this time, kids," he said. "You can hang out all you want later."

So that just meant that we'd have to throw our napkin ball bombs a little farther to hit each other.

After we were seated, Hunter threw the first one, right at my forehead.

"Open and read," he said.

So I did.

Dimple-Dunk 5000 = Complete! Check it out after dinner.

I gave Hunter a thumbs-up.

"What's with the thumbs-up?" Lola hollered from across the table.

"The Dimple Dunker is done. I'm going to check it out later. Wanna come?".

"What's done?" Kendall yelled from where she and Hunter were sitting with Aunt Kassie.

"The Dimple Dunker!" I yelled back.

Mom put her fingers in her ears. "This isn't working, Wayne.

I'm going to go deaf on Mother's Day. Please, let the kids sit together."

At her request, we all played musical chairs, and the pre-teen cousins ended up sitting together after all.

We had a great dinner. I couldn't tell what most of my family ordered, because everything was smothered in that heavenly gravy. I devoured some gourmet mac and cheese, and I ate way too many biscuits and cornbread for someone who also planned on ordering the s'mores dessert. We joked and laughed, Mamaw complimented the chef on his meatloaf, and both Ruby and my Uncle Josiah snorted milk out of their noses when we retold the T-Rex limbo story.

It was a perfect Carroway night out.

And then the Doonsberrys arrived.

I had to check twice, because at first it looked like a different family. Madison had on a lacey white dress, with pink low heels, and both Parker and his dad were wearing navy blue suits. A woman was with them. A tall blonde, with professionally done eye makeup. She wore a pink chiffon dress, white high heels, and a jeweled necklace with matching earrings that sparkled in the light as she walked toward their table. She sat down next to Parker on one side, and Mr. Doonsberry and Madison sat across from them. As soon as they were settled, the woman took out her phone and began scrolling.

Lola, who was now sitting next to me, nudged me with her elbow. "I bet that's her mom. She looks like a model. I love her dress."

I tried to look without them knowing, by taking a long

drink from my water and peeking through the bottom of the glass.

Mr. Doonsberry was trying to talk to the woman, but she just kept scrolling.

Parker tapped her arm and then pointed to his dad. She threw her phone down on the table, leaned back in her chair, and crossed her arms in front of her.

Madison attempted to hand her a menu, but she pushed it away and leaned forward to talk. Then the waiter came over, but she ignored him and kept talking.

By now, I had finished my glass of water, and the ice cubes were bonking me on the nose, so I had to look away for a few minutes.

"That's their mom," Hunter said. "Parker said she was coming to visit for Mother's Day. He seemed kind of nervous about the whole thing."

"I feel so sorry for Madison," Lola said. "She must really miss her mom."

I figured I could see better if I took a stroll.

"I'm going to the bathroom, be back in a sec."

I pushed back my chair, got up, and darted between support posts in the restaurant, each time peeking at the Doonsberry table. The waiter was succeeding in taking orders now, but Madison's dad looked upset.

Right as I reached the hallway that led to the bathroom, Parker's eyes met mine. I gave him a small wave and then disappeared into the ladies' room.

I didn't really have a reason to be in there, but Parker had seen me go in, so I needed to stay in there for a few minutes so that things looked legit. I popped into a stall, mostly so I could have some privacy to think about the scene I just witnessed in the restaurant.

Was that really Madison's mom?

I didn't have to wonder long, because pink and white heels came clacking into the bathroom.

"Liar!" Madison yelled. "You're *always* lying to me!"

"No, Madi, I didn't lie. Plans just changed, that's all. I would take you if I could, you know that."

I hopped up and stood on the toilet seat.

"You promised to take me! Tell your boss you promised!"

"Honey, that wouldn't do any good. This trip is just not going to be good for children."

"Well, isn't that convenient!"

The shoes clicked back and forth on the tile. Someone started the hand dryer.

"I'll take you to Paris next time, I promise."

Oh no, not the Paris trip. Madison was looking forward to that.

"DON'T promise me ANYTHING!" Madison was screaming now. "GO AWAY!"

Then, sobbing.

The heels clicked some more, toward the sink.

"Leave me alone," Madison said.

And then one set of heels—I was pretty sure it was the white ones—clicked out the door.

I stood there, on the toilet seat, wishing Madison would go out so I could escape, but also hoping that her mom would come back in to fix things with her daughter.

Neither of those things happened. Instead, Madison spoke.

"I know you're in there, Allie. I saw your family in the reserved room and I spotted your tacky camo loafers before you hopped up on the seat."

I jumped down, and pulled open the squeaky door. "Hey, Madison."

Madison entered the next stall, and pulled some toilet paper off the roll to wipe her eyes.

"What are the Carroways doing in a restaurant on Mother's Day, anyway? I thought you always had perfect homecooked family dinners, complete with prayers and stupid jokes and stuff."

Her shoulders heaved up and down.

"I'm really sorry about your Paris trip, Madison."

Madison wiped her nose. "I bet you had your phone, recording that whole scene, right? Whatever. You can put it on the Internet and then everyone will know that *my* family's a broken mess."

"No, I didn't. I would never do that."

Madison shrugged. "Go ahead. I couldn't care less." She headed to the door, but then turned back. "You can also post that I'll be returning all the fundraising money, because my dad can't put the winner on his show. He said something about some stupid clause in his contract."

"Oh, Madison . . ."

She walked out the door. I stood there, not knowing if I should go comfort her or push her face in a plate of gravy.

Then the door opened again.

"And one more thing," Madison said. "My dog's dead. Make sure you tell everyone that too."

CHAPTER 26

Turning Point

"Allie, is everything okay? You haven't been yourself since The Cracker Barrel."

Lola walked next to me, up the hill from the Lickety Split and then a few houses over to see Mr. Dimple's finished creation.

"Yeah, you didn't even eat your dessert," Hunter said. "Thanks for giving it to me, though." The boy still had a little marshmallow on his chin.

As we approached Mr. Dimple's yard, Ruby gasped and put her hand to her throat. "Is that it? It's huge!"

"I'm *not* goin' in there," Kendall said.

I tilted my head back to take in the whole view of the Dimple-Dunk 5000. It was black-and-green camo, and the target had an alligator face painted on it.

"It's perfect," I said. "We've never had anything this unique at the school carnival before. I'm sure we'll raise lots of money with this. Awesome job, Hunter."

Hunter smiled big. "I told you it was going to be amazing."

"But who are we gonna dunk?" Ruby asked. "I can't imagine dunking *any* of my friends in there. It would be too humiliating."

"Well. . . . how about enemies?" Kendall said. "I bet Lola'd pay some big bucks to dunk whoever stole her phone and posted that video on the Internet."

"Kendall! I would not."

Then she walked over, climbed up on a little step stool, and pushed on the alligator target. A lever gave way, and the seat that would be holding the "victim" dropped into the 5,000-gal-lon water container.

She grinned. "Okay, maybe for charity."

And that's when I got the idea.

It was actually Hunter's idea from the meeting, with a little tweaking.

That night, I texted Miss Lewis.

> Let's use our unpopularity to make some money. Dunk Tank and Pie-in-the-Face booths. Kids vote for the "victims." Are you game?

It only took ten seconds for her to respond:

> GAME ON.

CHAPTER 27

Reality Take Two

Lunker Law may have been the hottest new reality show on TV that season, but *Carried Away with the Carroways* had been on the longest—which meant we had built a good relationship with our directors and producers. And *sometimes* we could invite special guests on the show—if we asked real nice.

"Zeke? Can I talk to you at the break?" It was the night after Mother's Day, and Hunter, Kendall, and I were filming an outdoor golf scene with our dads using glow-in-the-dark balls.

Zeke winked. "Sure. We'll break after everyone putts out."

Twenty minutes, and ten lost balls later, I finally got to approach Zeke with my request.

"What's up, Allie-Oop? You tired of golf already?"

"Nah, I could golf all night."

Zeke smiled. "You're the best."

This was as good a time as ever. "Zeke, you know how I'm in charge of the year-end project at the middle school . . ."

"Yeah. Is that coming up? I was going to see if we could work that in to the show somehow."

"Well, it's actually next Saturday, and I'm in a little bit of a tight spot. I was wondering if you could help me out."

"What do you need, squirt?"

I took a deep breath, and told him the whole story. Including that Madison had obligated her dad to invite the winner of a drawing on his show.

Zeke crunched up his face. "Ooh. That's not good. It's his first season, so I'm sure they are playing things extra safe with the scripts."

"Well, that's why I was wondering—since we've been on a *few* seasons—can *we* do anything? Can we invite Mr. Doonsberry on our show and then have the winner appear with him?"

"You mean like *Lunker Law* meets the Carroways?"

"Yeah. That would allow the school to keep the fundraising money, and the winner would be able to be on TV with the *Lunker Law* guy. I think they might accept that—if we could do it."

"Hmmmm." Zeke rubbed his chin. "We don't have a lot of time to plan, and I'm not sure the producers will go for it."

I placed my putter up on my shoulders, and hung my hands over the shaft. "Zeke, I'll do anything. I'll fish, I'll clean fish guts. I'll wear a tiara and full camo *while* cleaning fish guts. Please . . ."

Zeke took the putter from me and pretended to line up and hit a ball toward the hole. Then he looked up at me.

"You drive a hard bargain, Allie Carroway. I'll see what I can do."

Two days came and went, and I still didn't have an answer from Zeke. The final steering committee meeting would be tomorrow and I wanted to pitch my idea for the two shows merging and about having a "Dunk-and-Pie" voting campaign.

So, while I waited, I spent another afternoon, pacing back and forth in the Lickety Split, reading out loud all the Bible verses that Lola had finally hung up.

"Be still and know that I am God."

I read that, and kept pacing.

"The Lord is my light and my salvation, whom shall I fear?"

No one, so why did I feel afraid right now?

"Be strong and courageous . . ."

I tried that, and it got me elected to head up this crazy project.

Then I remembered Mom's words.

"Your enemies want you to think you're a loser, but don't believe them! You're God's precious daughter—case closed!"

I grabbed my head with both hands and pushed, as if that would suppress the negative thoughts rolling around in my head. Then I lay down on the beanbag and looked up.

"Give all your cares and worries to God . . ."

Keep looking up, Allie.

"Okay, but you gotta help me, God!" I yelled that maybe a little too loud, but I wanted to make sure he'd hear.

A boy's voice rang out from the balcony of the Lickety Split.

"There you are! We've been looking for you."

Hunter poked his head in the door. "We need you over at the house for a family meeting in ten minutes!"

I sat up and tried to smooth my hair. A family meeting? With the *whole* family?

When I arrived at the house, it did look like the whole family was there. They were gathered out on the patio, and Aunt Kassie and my mom served iced tea and scones to a smiling crowd. This had to be a good meeting if there were scones.

"Well, lookie here, the guest of honor has arrived." Papaw came over and led me by the arm to a patio chair with puffy orange cushions. "We have some things to tell you, Allie-girl."

Aunt Kassie placed a cup of tea in my hand.

"Thanks," I said, and I took a huge gulp.

Zeke and the film crew came in from the side of the house. He leaned down and whispered in my ear. "I hope you meant what you said about the camo and the fish guts—'cause you're gonna owe me big."

Then he addressed the crowd.

"Clear your schedules, folks, because next Saturday, *Carried Away with the Carroways* is going on location—to the Ouachita Middle School Bark Fest Carnival and Dog Show. We'll be filming for an episode entitled *Lunker Law* meets *Carried Away with the Carroways*, to be aired later this year. But we'll also be goin' live on our FriendClips page during the whole event, accepting online donations. One hundred percent of the proceeds will go to the West Monroe Animal Shelter."

Everyone clapped.

"We should be able to make enough money to tear that old place down and build a brand-new one," Lola said.

I could hardly believe what I was hearing.

Mamaw stepped forward and handed me a list of family members with jobs written next to their names. "We'll do whatever you need, Allie-girl, but here are some suggestions, in case you hadn't thought of them." She winked. "I told you, you can always count on your family."

I scanned the list, and laughed out loud when I saw the job title scrawled next to my little cousin Chase's name:

Doggy-Poop Scooper.

No, I hadn't thought of that.

CHAPTER 28

And the Winner is . . .

I could barely sleep the night of May 26th. And even when I did doze off, I dreamed about dogs. The Bark Fest was the next day, and as Miss Lewis had said, "The outcome will speak for itself."

Or, perhaps it would bark for itself.

And it must be true what they say about dogs sensing when something is up, because that morning, all the dogs in Aunt Kassie and Uncle Wayne's house—Hazel Mae, Eleanor Rigby, and T-Rex—were a bundle of energy—licking and jumping and tearing around the house chasing each other.

Kendall chased Ellie around the living room trying to put her pink camo bandanna on.

"Come here, crazy girl! You can't have a naked neck for the dog show!" Kendall finally gave up and plopped down on the couch. "I'll have to put it on her in the car."

"If you can get her in the car," I said, and I shifted my legs into super-speed mode so I could catch up to Hazel Mae.

"Haha, gotcha!" I slipped the pink camo bandanna around her neck, and then I waved my index finger at her. "Okay, here are the rules. You stay away from that red-headed Doonsberry girl, got it? And if you see anyone named "Frenelope," feel free to chew on her ankle like it's a bone."

"Allie!"

I looked up the stairs and saw Mom, staring down.

"Sorry, Mom. I guess I'm still working out that forgiveness thing."

"T-Rex is ready!" Hunter appeared at the top of the steps, holding the little corgi, whose brown-and-white coloring sort of makes him look like a hamster. "Wait till you see what he and Chief have cooked up for the dog trick competition."

I laughed. "T-Rex and *Chief*? That's gonna be like an elephant and mouse show."

"Precisely," Hunter said. "We'll be using their size differential to wow the crowd."

I looked down at my sports watch, and a squirt of adrenaline lifted me off the stairs.

"People! It's time! We gotta be out of here in five minutes!"

All members of both the families living under Aunt Kassie and Uncle Wayne's roof came thundering out of the house and piled into several vehicles. Thankfully, all our dogs were small, so we could hold them on our laps. I wondered how Parker was going to transport Chief, and then my thoughts went straight to Madison and what she had said to me in the bathroom at The Cracker Barrel.

And one more thing. My dog is dead.

I pulled Hazel Mae in close and snuggled her against my cheek. "If I ever lost you, it would surely tear a huge dog-shaped hole in my heart."

Then I remembered what Mamaw had said about Madison.

"She's got a God-shaped hole in her heart."

Wow. Madison has a God-shaped hole, *and* a dog-shaped hole.

Maybe you can do something about that, Allie.

That quiet voice speaking to me in my spirit as we pulled into the parking lot of the school shook me up a little. What did God want *me* to do? This girl had been working to destroy me ever since she moved into my old house. I had already tried to patch things up—to make a little peace, but she obviously wasn't interested.

Miss Lewis met me outside our SUV.

She had a pink camo hat on, and her hair was in two braids. She also wore an army-green tank top, and dark-grey cargo shorts. She looked much younger, but more like a sergeant than ever before. She was also holding a manila envelope.

"It took you long enough to get here, Carroway."

She *sounded* more like a sergeant now too.

"Are you ready to see the results of the vote?"

She held the envelope out for me to take it. I placed Hazel Mae on the back seat of the SUV and opened it.

The "vote" had been Hunter's idea for picking who should go in the Dimple-Dunk 5000. But it wasn't until the other day that I realized Miss Lewis and I could take advantage of our "unpopularity,"—and the unfortunate Lewis-Beetle incident—to bring in some "big" money. And *this* money was not going to be for the animal shelter.

Last Monday, I had talked Mr. Langley into letting me get on the intercom to address the whole school.

"Attention, Ouachita Eagles, this is Allie Carroway."

I imagined groaning going on in the classrooms at that moment, because—though Miss Lewis had ripped up the petition, I still had most of the student body annoyed with me.

"The funds are piling up for support of the Bark Fest Carnival and Dog Show, and I am certain we will exceed our monetary goals to benefit the animal shelter."

I hoped there might be cheers in the classroom now, but no matter. I continued.

"As you all know, Mrs. Mellon's infant daughter Bethany is racking up tons of medical bills. I have a suggestion for a way we can help little Bethany pay some of those bills so she can start saving for college."

"I can't wait to hear this!" Mr. Langley said.

"At the end of the carnival this Saturday, we will have two special booths, located right next to each other. One will be the Dimple-Dunk 5000—the largest dunk tank this side of the Mississippi. Next to the Dimple-Dunk 5000 will be a pie-throwing booth, called the "Lewis-Beetle Cure." For two hours, you can dunk and throw at the person in each booth for only ten dollars for three throws. It's for a good cause, people! And you, the student body of Ouachita Middle School, will vote on one faculty member, and one student to be the targets in those booths. So, I need to ask you . . . who do you want to see dunked and pied? Cast your votes during lunch all this week. The faculty member and student with the most votes will see how much money they can rake in for the 'Mini-Mellon' Fund."

I switched off the intercom and glanced over at the Mr. Langley, who gave me a sympathetic look.

"They *might* vote for Jared. Or Paige," he said.

I laughed. "That's highly unlikely, considering my current track record. But *you* might win the faculty vote."

Mr. Langley pointed two index fingers back at me. "Highly unlikely, Miss Carroway. Especially when the booth is named "The Lewis-Beetle Cure.""

Miss Lewis would win—no doubt. My brother Cody even promised to travel home from college to throw a few pies.

"Bring all your money," I had told him over the phone.

"Open the envelope, Allie!" Hunter jumped up and down behind me.

"Yeah, the suspense is killing us." Kendall reached over and tried to take the envelope, but I pulled it back.

"Really, people? Suspense? Are you kidding me?"

The only suspense for me was wondering if my landslide victory margin would be greater than when I was elected SPM.

I opened the envelope, and pulled out a single piece of paper.

The word at the top was in all caps:

UNANIMOUS.

And then there were two names:

Miss Lewis
Allie Carroway

I turned back toward my cousins. "Unanimous? I certainly didn't think it would be unanimous! Did *you two* vote for *me*?"

Hunter shrugged. "It was for Mini-Mellon, Allie."

Kendall backed up, eyes wide. "You *wanted* to be in the tank, right?"

And then both of my cousins took off running, with their dogs, toward the big white tent in the center of the carnival.

"Oh, you are sooooo dead when I catch you!" I yelled.

I turned, and Miss Lewis had her hand out, ready to shake mine.

"Good work, Carroway. This will be a year-end project to remember."

CHAPTER 29

Bark Fest

The carnival and all the dog show activities cranked away with record crowds from 10:00 a.m. until 1:30 p.m. People ate tons of food from the various food booths, bought all of Lola's crafts, lined up to play in the game booths—even the silly Carroway ones—and they just about cleared out everything from Mamaw's bake sale. Mr. Doonsberry and his *Lunker Law* boat were set up at the north end of the carnival grounds, and a line of people wrapped all the way around to get autographs and selfies with Mr. Doonsberry, and to take pictures of themselves in the boat. Ruby ran the dog show all morning like a champ. It was fun to see the excitement on the faces of kids walking their dogs around the grounds with different color award ribbons hanging from their necks.

The "Spectacular Dog Trick Competition" was about to begin.

Ruby's cute voice rang out on the loudspeaker. "All those who registered for the dog trick competition, please proceed to the east side of the white tent for check-in. All others please find a seat in the grandstand. The contest will start in thirty minutes!"

I reached down to pet my little fur ball. "Sorry I didn't have time to teach you anything, Hazel Mae. But maybe you can help me out later . . ."

"Allie! Have you seen Parker?" Hunter ran up to me, all out of breath.

I looked out in the distance, and no—I didn't see Parker. I did see his big horse-dog, and a bobbing head behind it that was probably Parker.

I pointed over Hunter's shoulder.

"I think he's coming."

Hunter turned, yelled, "Goliath is here!" and then ran to meet his trick partners.

My mom came up behind me and put her arm around my shoulders. "Well, Allie, it looks like this year-end project turned out okay after all. I'm glad you didn't let your enemies get the best of you."

That reminded me. I hadn't see Madison all day.

Of all people, I would expect her to be here, soaking up all the attention.

Mom and I walked over to the tent, and sat in a reserved seat in the front row of the grandstand. As soon as the Dog Trick Spectacular was over, I was scheduled to pull the name of the winner of who would be appearing with us on the *Lunker Law* meets *Carried Away with the Carroways* episode. We would also be introducing Mr. Felix, who would accept a big cardboard check with the estimated amount raised for the animal shelter.

But first, it was an hour of hilarity watching the dogs of West Monroe perform.

First, we had the Frisbee flyers—with Uncle Saul leading the way. Dogs of all shapes and sizes chased the Frisbees, and they were so cute—especially this one little white bulldog who got tired and lay down in the middle of the crowd—his feet sprawled out behind him. His owner—one of our school football players—had to come and drag him off.

Since most of the dogs could jump but couldn't catch, Ruby's dog, Max, won that contest—hands down. His prize was a golden Frisbee (not real gold, of course).

Next came the "real" competition, and the dogs did not disappoint. Quite a few performed routines with rolls and jumps, walking on hind legs and barking on command. Lola's dog, Monet, held a paintbrush in her mouth and crafted a masterpiece. I don't have any idea what the picture was supposed to be—but if you placed it in an art gallery tomorrow, people would flock to it and call it a classic.

Rachel Long's Chiweenies performed a comedy act—at least that's what it turned out to be. She had dressed them up like hot dogs—with bun costumes—and they ran around with empty ketchup and mustard dispensers in their mouths, jumping up on people's laps—but mostly barking.

Ellie and Kendall even entered the competition. Kendall played the guitar, and Ellie sat up on a stool—with daisies clipped up above her ears—and barked a short song.

I think it was the beginning of the Parker love song, and when their act was finished, I formed a little heart with my fingers. Kendall saw me, blushed, and put a hand over her face.

The final trick of the show was next. The elephant and the mouse.

Parker, Hunter, and T-Rex walked in, crouched behind Chief. Then they popped out from behind him, and Hunter began his announcement.

"Ladies and gentlemen, boys and girls, some of you may have heard from your students that my dog T-Rex here had some trouble performing the famous Carroway Catapult. Well, that is no longer. All he needed was the right partner. So, now—for your enjoyment—sit back and be amazed as Chief and T-Rex perform—The David and Goliath!

Suspenseful music began playing in the background as Parker dragged out a mini-trampoline and Hunter grabbed a hula-hoop. Then Hunter placed T-Rex on Chief's back!

Oh, no.

I put my hands over my eyes, but parted them a bit so I could see. Chief began to run around the circle in the middle of the tent. He slowed a few times when T-Rex looked like he was going to fall off.

The crowd laughed.

As soon as T-Rex regained his footing, Chief started running faster. The third time around the circle, Chief had really picked up speed—which surprised me.

This trick could really end with T-Rex on the moon.

Chief ran around the circle again, but this time changed his direction at the end and pointed toward the mini-tramp.

Mom reached over and squeezed my hand, her eyes wide.

Chief finally made it within three feet of the trampoline, and jumped.

The crowd gasped.

Will that thing hold him?

It did, and when he bounced on it, T-Rex flew off his back— not quite to the moon—but at least eight feet up and five feet over. His little legs flipped around in the air. At that point, Parker raised the hoop up, and T-Rex dropped right through!

And Hunter—with a huge smile on his face—caught Doggy-Short-Legs, much to the delight of the crowd.

It was a "Standing O" moment—with thunderous applause that lasted several minutes—which made it pretty obvious who would win first prize at the Ouachita Middle School Spectacular Dog Trick Competition.

CHAPTER 30

Dunks & Pies

During the prize ceremony, I checked my phone for two things: the amount donated through Madison's FriendClips page, and the amount being pledged on the *Carried Away with the Carroways* live feed.

We were almost to fifty-thousand dollars! Goosebumps broke out all over my head, shoulders, and arms.

Thank you, God.

Mr. Langley was giving a speech, but I had trouble being still for that. I just wanted to turn a few cartwheels to get rid of some energy.

Mom nudged me with her elbow. "I think it's your turn to get up there."

Mr. Langley must have called for me, because the crowd was silent, and he and Miss Lewis were standing up there waiting for something.

I jumped up and ran to the front. Miss Lewis handed me a microphone.

"Seems we still have to work on your punctuality, Carroway."

I faced the crowd, and the goosebumps came back. I had dreamed of this day for two years. And yes, most of the last two months had been a nightmare, but *this* . . . this is what it was all about.

I called for Mr. Felix to join us, and as he did, Jared Strickland and Paige Wright brought up the big check. It was for $50,000.

I did my best to speak, even though I had a big lump in my throat.

"Thank you, Ouachita Middle School, for your time, your support, and your generosity. I love living in this community, and one of my favorite places to visit is our local animal shelter. It's already the best one around, but with the funds that have been raised through your efforts, it will now be even better!"

Everyone in the crowd clapped as Jared and Paige handed Mr. Felix the check. Mr. Felix beamed, shook everyone's hand, put his hand to his heart, and bowed to the crowd. Then he dragged the check off, and Jared, Paige, and Mr. Langley followed. That left me and Miss Lewis to conduct the drawing, and to announce the "victims" that would soon be pied and dunked—as if anyone wondered.

Miss Lewis walked off to the side and pushed in a barrel on wheels that had the names of everyone who had donated at least two-hundred dollars in goods or services. The thing was full. I had to give Madison credit for that.

But, *where was she*?

"Okay, people—can you give me a drumroll?" The audience slapped their hands on their laps, and Miss Lewis turned the barrel round and round. Finally, she stopped it, and opened the little door so I could shove my hand in.

I pulled out a folded slip of paper, and my hands shook a little.

"The winner of our drawing will make a cameo appearance on a special show that combines both *Lunker Law* and *Carried Away with the Carroways*. Doesn't that sound like fun?"

The crowd clapped some more.

"And the winner is . . ."

I opened the paper and stared at the name.

Seriously.

I could hardly make my mouth say it.

"Saul Carroway."

Uncle Saul jumped up from the back of the grandstand.

"Yes!" he pumped his fists up and down and yelled, "I love *Lunker Law*! That guy's hilarious!"

All my aunts and uncles in the front row shook their heads. Uncle Wayne stood up and held his palms to the sky.

"But, Uncle Saul, you're *already* going to be on this show!"

"I am?"

"Saul," Aunt Kassie said. "You're on *all* the shows."

Uncle Saul scratched his head. "I guess you're right."

It was another awkward moment, but I was starting to get used to them.

"Well," Miss Lewis said, "Since he *did* donate, and we picked his name—he's the winner. Perhaps we should let him choose someone *he'd* like to invite on the show."

I was going to ask the crowd what they thought, but then I figured, hey—I'm the Student Project Manager—so maybe I should act like it.

"Saul, is there an OMS student you'd like to be on the show?"

Saul came down to stand by me. "Yes, there is. I'd like to pick that kid over there—Joey Sanger. We stood in the *Lunker Law* line for an hour together, and I'm telling ya—he's a true fan!"

Joey—my friend since kindergarten who had done nothing but talk about the *Lunker Law* boat for the last two months—came down from the grandstand, weaving side-to-side—looking like he was going to faint.

"I-I'm gonna be on TV?"

"Yes," I said, "you are."

He grinned ear-to-ear.

"I'm glad I voted for you, Allie."

Yeah, I bet you voted for me. Both times!

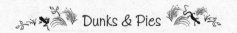

The rest of the ceremony was anti-climactic after the Uncle Saul mix-up. As soon as I announced that it would be me in the Dimple-Dunk 5000 and Miss Lewis in the Lewis-Beetle Pie Booth, people tore out of the tent and began to line up to take their shots.

The lines were even longer than the one for the *Lunker Law* boat!

"Maybe we'll pay off Bethany's medical bills *and* cover her college tuition," Miss Lewis said.

"Game on," I said.

I think we used up all the whipped cream in West Monroe that day. Miss Lewis tried *not* to smile when her former students wound up and threw pies at her. She heckled them mercilessly when they missed.

"That's one out of four, you slacker! If I remember right, you scored 25% on all your tests too! I *dare* you to try again!" And they shelled out another ten bucks and jumped back in line.

She *threatened* the current students. "Hit me with that pie, and expect tons of homework next week!" It didn't stop anybody. They shelled out their parents' bucks and jumped back in line.

"Where are people getting all this money?" I yelled. I heard Miss Lewis start to answer, but them some wise guy hit the alligator target and sent me ker-splashing into the Dimple-Dunk 5000. I held my breath and swam around, giving people evil stares from the other side of the window.

So this was what fish in aquariums felt like.

At one point, I yelled over to Mom to bring Hazel Mae in the Dunker with me.

"She loves to swim," I said.

As soon as I had her with me, people started missing the target. I think they were distracted by her cute little face, *and* her fake sneezing.

It didn't matter to me. We collected ten dollars for Mini-Mellon whether they hit the target or not.

At the one-hour mark, I checked out my fingers. They were wrinkled up like raisins.

"We're at $5,000 already!" Mr. Langley hollered over from the table where the huge money bottle was filling up. "People are putting in more than we're asking!"

"Hey—I didn't spend the last ten years making my students mad for nothin'," Miss Lewis said.

The next one up in her line was my brother Cody. He'd rolled in from college that afternoon.

"Hey, bro! How come you're not in my line?"

Cody balanced a pie in his hand and closed one eye to aim at Miss Lewis.

"I can always pick on you. But right now, it's payback time!"

Miss Lewis laughed. "Payback? For what? Straightening you up?"

Cody chucked the pie, and it hit Miss Lewis right on the nose.

"Yeah! That's for straightening me up! And the next one will be for forcing me to work hard."

"I bet you can't even afford another pie," Miss Lewis yelled.

"Stay tuned, I'm coming back around a few more times."

Cody threw in thirty bucks and ran to the back of the line.

"This is too easy, Carroway." Miss Lewis licked some cream

off her upper lip. "And I'm going to have baby soft skin when this is over."

Right as she said that, someone hit my target, and I kersplashed again—this time with Hazel Mae. She barked and sneezed and doggy-paddled around the top of the water while I tried to grab on to the ladder to take me back up to my perch. I laughed so hard, I almost peed in the Dimple-Dunk 5000, which would have made it the Dimple-Dunk 5001.

The next hour zipped by, and people were *still* in line.

"I didn't know we had so many 'fans'," I said.

Mr. Langley came over and shook his head. "We have to cut this off at some point."

But Miss Lewis and I just looked at each other and grinned.

"No way," I said.

"We'll cut it off when they're out of money," Miss Lewis added.

And that took two more hours.

CHAPTER 31

A Dog-Shaped Hole

The next morning at church, my fingers were still raisin-like. But it was worth it—even if they stayed like that forever—because we raised a little over $10,000 for the Mini-Mellon fund. Right after church, we visited the Mellons to give them the good news.

"Well, the tenth-anniversary year-end project didn't happen quite how I planned." Mrs. Mellon sat in the lounge of the hospital, squeezing a little teddy bear. "But in a way, this is so much better."

"I can't believe all the support we got from everyone in the community," I said. "And the steering committee really stepped up—even after that whole petition thing."

"I knew they'd come around," Mrs. Mellon brushed a little tear from her cheek. "Deep down, I think everyone knows what a caring person you are, Allie."

Not everyone.

But I was still working on that.

"Okay, let her know you're here, Hazel Mae."

I grabbed Hazel Mae's paw and pushed it on the doorbell.

A few seconds later, Madison Doonsberry opened her front door.

She was wearing casual clothes. Tan shorts, and a light

blue tank top. Her hair was gathered up in a high ponytail—
and no bracelets on this Sunday afternoon.

"Oh. Hello, Hazel Mae," Madison said. "Are you wanting to
use the backyard?"

I stifled a laugh.

"Not today," I said.

"Then how can I help you?"

Lord, I *hope this works*.

"Well, we wanted to get your opinion on something."

She raised her eyebrows. "You want *my* opinion?"

I nodded. "Yeah. Mr. Felix is trying to find homes for a few
of his dogs so he can make room in the shelter while they're
remodeling. He wasn't sure what to do with one particular dog,
so I asked if I could bring it over here to see what you thought."

Madison rolled her eyes, and stepped out from the door.

"Whatever," she said. "Where is it?"

"It's in a crate, in the back of the SUV." I walked out to the
street where Mom was parked. She looked out the window at
me and winked.

I pulled up the liftgate, and asked Madison to open the
crate. The golden retriever puppy whimpered a little, but then
charged forward and began licking Madison on the chin.

Madison scooped the puppy up in her arms and buried her
face in its neck.

"You're so soft and adorable," she said, and then she looked
at me. "Is it a girl?"

I nodded. "Yep."

Madison was speechless. She hugged that little thing for a
few minutes, and then she sat up on the back of the tailgate.
The puppy stayed in her lap.

"We missed you at the Bark Fest," I said.

Madison kept petting the puppy and didn't look up.

"I just wasn't feeling it. I'm sorry."

"It's okay. All the work you did paid off big-time."

Madison grinned, sort of. "I heard. Thanks for getting us out of that fundraising jam. That could have been a real mess."

"But, hey—it wasn't, right? I think we all made a really great team."

"Yeah."

Madison picked the puppy up so she could look closely at her face. "You remind me of my dog, Millie. I got her when she was about your size. I miss her very much."

Then she jumped off the tailgate and put the puppy back in the crate. "I think this dog would make a perfect pet for someone."

"How about you?"

Madison's eyes grew wide. "Me? Is that even an option?"

I smiled. "Sure. My mom called your dad, and he said he's all for it. He said since you're not going to Paris this summer, you'll have plenty of time to take care of a puppy."

Madison stepped back from the crate and put both hands on her cheeks.

"This is unbelievable! I would LOVE to take this puppy. But, I'd have to find someone to care for her when I'm at camp."

I gulped. "You're going to camp?"

Madison put her hand on her forehead and shook her head. "Yeah. Daddy signed me up to go to some Christian thing during the last week of June. I'm not too happy about it. But, if I get to keep this little sweetie, I'll have something to look forward to when I get home."

She smiled and reached in for more puppy snuggles.

"Allie, I can't believe you brought me a dog. I haven't exactly been nice to you."

I shrugged. "I know. You've had a rough year."

Madison's eyes filled up. "It's been horrible. Sometimes I feel like my heart is breaking apart—just like my family."

"I'm really sorry, Madison. And I meant what I said before. I hope we can start over and be friends someday."

Madison grinned, for real this time. "I'd like that."

Whoa. Miracle!

I reached out and roughed up the puppy's neck fur.

"And I think this little one can help heal your heart. Dogs are pretty amazing."

"Yes, they are," Madison said.

"Do you want to take these two for a walk next Saturday? I know Hazel Mae would love to run over here in the morning."

Madison laughed.

"I bet she would."

"I'm proud of you, Allie," Mom said on the drive home. "It took strong character to forgive Madison, after all she put you through."

"Thanks, Mom."

"And the dog idea was brilliant."

"That was easy. Mr. Felix had an extra dog, and Madison had a dog-shaped hole in her heart."

And God, I'll leave it up to you to work on that other hole.

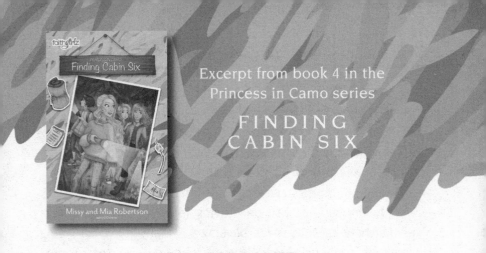

FINDING CABIN SIX

CHAPTER ONE

Necessities

"Duct tape, rope, scissors, hanging vines, monkeys . . ." I scratched my head and scanned the shelves and other flat surfaces in the bedroom I share with my cousin, Kendall.

"Can you think of anything else we need?"

Kendall pulled some super glue from her desk drawer and then crammed a purple ukulele into the medium-sized suitcase we had set aside for "camp essentials."

"There." She sat on her bed, scrunched her lips together, and rested her fist on her chin. "What about flower garlands?"

I pointed to my teeny white poof-ball dog, Hazel Mae. She and Kendall's black miniature poodle, Ellie, were playing tug-of-war with the garlands.

"Good luck getting those away from them in one piece."

Kendall jumped off her bed and ran toward the dogs.

"Ellie! Drop!"

At the sound of Kendall's command, Ellie and Hazel Mae disappeared out the door with the garlands.

Kendall threw her hands up in the air. "We need those if we plan on being cabin champs again this year."

"I'm sure there are more in the boxes downstairs. I saw some inflatable birds and geckos too."

Kendall sat back on the bed and crossed her arms. "There are a million boxes stacked up down there."

My family—who had been living with Kendall's family for a long nine months—was packing to finally move into our newly-built, allergen-free home on a brand-new street in our neighborhood—Timbuktu Court.

Our move-in date was planned for next Monday—two days after we were scheduled to return from our week at summer camp.

"Come on." I grabbed Kendall's hand to tug her off her bed. "I'll help you dig through the boxes."

But we didn't move, because Kendall wrapped me up in a tight hug.

"I don't want you to move, Allie."

I laughed and tried to pry her arms from around me. "Yes, you *do*. And I'll only be five minutes away."

At the top of the stairs, we ran into my mom, who was carrying an overloaded laundry basket. She pushed us backward into our room and dumped the load of socks and underwear on my bed.

"I hope you girls intend to pack clothes and toiletries too." She glanced down at the suitcase with the twenty monkey eyes staring back at her.

"What in the world do you need *those* for?"

"Mom—everyone knows you need monkeys at camp."

"We're creatin' a rainforest environment," Kendall said. "We're goin' for cabin champs three years in a row, and décor is one of the top things they judge."

Mom began sorting socks from the mound. "And what if you girls *aren't* in the same cabin this year?"

I put my hands on my hips.

"That's *not* gonna happen."

Mom shook her head. "Well, okay. I'm just preparing you for the possibility—I don't want to hear you griping if you end up separated."

"We *have* to be together. This is our last week as roomies! Plus, we've written our cheer and everything." Kendall grabbed a couple of socks off the bed and swung them around like pom-poms.

"We're the best, and we will thrive, 'cause Jesus is alive in Cabin Five!"

Mom raised her eyebrows. "And how do you know you'll be in Cabin *Five*?"

"We've worked our way up," I said. "We're the oldest now, so we rule. That's all."

"But there are *lots* of girls your age, and last time I counted, there were only nine camper beds in Cabin Five. So, clearly *someone* isn't going to rule."

Kendall plopped the cheer socks back on the bed. "Yeah, too bad for them."

Right then my phone rang. The caller ID popped up a name: Madison Doonsberry.

I sighed. "It's Madison . . . again. She probably needs more packing advice. She's never been to a summer camp before."

"Tell her we could use some more monkeys," Kendall said.

Fiery redhead Madison Doonsberry and I got off to a rocky start last November when her family moved into my old house. She seemed to hate me for some reason, so I secretly referred to her as "Mad-girl," and tried to avoid her—kind of like how I avoid eating peanuts—to *survive*. But then, through a painful set of circumstances, God showed me that Madison didn't need someone to make fun of her or avoid her—she needed someone to care. And after a *lot* of prayer, I decided to try that—but slowly, and in small doses. Then, Madison found out she and I were both going to be at the same camp the last week in June, and she'd been calling me at least three times a day since Wednesday.

So much for small doses.

I poked the "answer" button on my phone and put her on speaker with me and Kendall.

"Hey, Madison. Are you still packing?"

A little puppy yelp came from the speaker.

"Petunia, stop chewing on the curtains!"

Petunia is Madison's golden retriever puppy.

"Allie, how many pairs of shoes should I bring? Petunia's chewed up most of mine."

I laughed. "That's fine. Chewed-up shoes are the best ones to bring. They're gonna get wet and dirty anyway."

"Petunia!"

Things went quiet on the other end of the line for a minute. Then Madison returned, out of breath.

"Wet *and* dirty? Why?"

Kendall laughed. "Camp. That's why."

"But it's a *Christian* camp, so there's less dirt, right? Doesn't everyone just sit around and make sweet crafts and sing hymns?"

"Ha! That's the funniest thing I've ever heard, Madison. Hang on a minute, I have to jot that one down in my journal."

"Don't tease me, Allie Carroway—and be truthful. How much dirt are we really talking about here?"

"Madison—there's dirt *everywhere*. In fact, bring dirt-colored clothes. And lots of socks."

"How many exactly?"

"At least three pairs for each day. And two pairs of shoes for the week. One to wear while the other dries out."

"Oh, yuck!"

Silence on the other end again.

"Madison? Are you still there?"

"Yes. I'm hugging Petunia and trying not to cry. Allie—I'm not sure I'll survive this week."

"Sure, you will. You're a bayou girl now, remember?"

I heard a loud sigh on the other end.

"Yes, I remember. In fact—it's my daily nightmare. Allie, will you help me when I'm at camp? I'm nervous. And I don't understand all that Christian stuff either. The packing list says I'm supposed to bring a Bible, and I don't even have one. Well, there is one on a stand in our living room. But it's the size of a small suitcase."

"I'll bring you a Bible."

"Oh, thank you, thank you, thank you!" Madison then began talking to her puppy. "Petunia, I'm going to miss you so much!"

"Okay, well . . . bye, Madison."

I hung up and lay down on my bed. I clasped my hands, raising them toward the ceiling.

"Kendall, *please* pray—with all your might—that Madison Doonsberry is *not* assigned to our cabin."

Kendall shook her head. "Nuh-uh. Lately, every time I ask God for somethin', he says no. I think *you* should ask instead."

"And *why* shouldn't Madison be in your cabin?"

Mom had returned with more laundry and glared in my direction.

I propped myself up on my elbows. "She's just not the camper type, Mom. And that means she'll be clingy and whiny. This is my last year at middle-school camp, and I don't want to spend it babysitting Madison Doonsberry."

"Well, it sounds like *you* have a little selfish streak going on." Mom set the laundry basket beside me on the bed and pulled an envelope from the top of the load. "According to this, it may be your last year at camp, *period*." She handed it over to me.

I opened it, and pulled out a letter to my parents from Lindsey Roth, our close family friend, and director of Camp 99 Pines.

Dear Camp 99 Pines Alumni,

We are eagerly awaiting your arrival next week to celebrate the Camp 99 Pines' 50th year anniversary! Enclosed you will find your tickets to the gala—to be held under the stars on everyone's favorite recreation field two. It's going to be a fabulous night, with three hundred in attendance!

Attached you will find a parking map for Friday evening. Also, for those arriving a day early, we are offering lunch and a tour of the camp at noon—when our middle-school students will be in session.

The next part of the letter made my heart hurt.

As I wrap up this letter, I am compelled to ask you to pray about the future of Camp 99 Pines. Founder and owner—Audrey Gables—is suffering from Alzheimer's Disease, and has been admitted to a local care facility. Her son, Patterson Gables, has put the property up for sale, and a housing developer has already offered a sum that is over the asking price—one that we on the camp board cannot match at this time.

Our camp is booked for the summer, so we will continue to operate, but if nothing changes, our last week as a Christian camp will be the week of August 9th. Until then, we are . . .

Trusting in the God of all Hope,

Lindsay Roth
Director, Camp 99 Pines

"Till all the lost have been found."

"Allie—your face! What's wrong?" Kendall jumped up off her bed and grabbed the letter out of my hand. "What does it say?"

"It says that the camp is up for sale," Mom said.

"For sale? Why?"

I pointed to the shocking paragraph.

"Audrey Gables' son wants to turn it into a neighborhood, I guess."

"A neighborhood? We've got plenty of neighborhoods!" Kendall stomped one foot on the floor. "Camp 99 Pines is historic—they can't sell it!"

"Can the Carroways buy it?" I turned to my mom. "We've got money from doing the show, right?"

My whole family stars in a reality TV show called *Carried Away with the Carroways*. It all started when I was about seven, and it focuses on our life in the Louisiana bayou—particularly my dad and uncles and their duck hunting escapades.

"Do we have enough to buy the camp?" Kendall looked over at Mom, who was now sitting on my bed, matching up pairs of socks.

"Maybe," she said. "But owning a camp is a huge undertaking. And something tells me that this situation is a lot more complicated than someone else simply buying the camp."

"What's complicated?" I said. "We buy it, and it stays a Christian camp."

Mom took the letter from Kendall and shook her head. "It says right here that Audrey's son, Patterson, is in charge now, and it appears he has other interests. Maybe he's not even a believer."

"With parents who own a Christian camp? That impossible."

"It's possible in any family, Allie," Mom said.

"Well, either way, I think the Carroways should pay a visit to this Patterson Gables person." I balled up a few socks and threw them in my suitcase.

Mom's eyes opened wide. "Allie, I think that's enough socks."

"Yeah, but I could be mucking around in the mud this week, looking for ways to save the camp."

Mom pointed her index finger toward my chin.

"Listen here, girl. You're going as a *camper*, not a crusader. Got that? Let the grown-ups figure this out. You just pray."

I didn't change my expression at all.

"Allie . . ."

"I'll pray," I said.

"And take *good* care of Madison. Put yourself in her shoes. How would you like to be treated as if it were your first year at camp?"

I nodded. "Yes, ma'am." I reached into my top dresser drawer and pulled out more socks. "She'll need these."

A long pause. Then Mom continued.

"You'll be out in the bayou with snakes and alligators. No mucking, sneaking, hiking, peeking, or even *thinking* about lurking around where you don't belong."

"Yes, ma'am."

She took a deep breath...